ANGEL'S SNARE

The murderer watched the body's almost graceful progress until it reached the roof of the nave. There, it teetered on the edge, nearly lodged in the guttering, then fell further like a monstrous bird shot with an arrow. It hit the ground below and spread out, very still, sprawling as if its arms and legs were carefully placed in some strange display. In the grey moonlight, its robe showed black against the stony ground, almost like the wings of an angel of death.

"Useless then, useless now," the murderer said, then stepped back inside the tower and felt a careful way down to the foot of the ladder.

Have you read the other books in this series?

The JOSLIN de LAY MYSTERIES

ANGEL'S SNARE

DENNIS HAMLEY

■SCHOLASTIC

Scholastic Children's Books,
Commonwealth House, 1–19 New Oxford Street,
London WC1A 1NU, UK
a division of Scholastic Ltd
London ~ New York ~ Toronto ~ Sydney ~ Auckland
Mexico City ~ New Delhi ~ Hong Kong

First published in the UK by Scholastic Ltd, 2001

ISBN 0 439 01371 2

Typeset by Falcon Oast Graphic Art
Printed by Cox and Wyman Ltd, Reading, Berks.

10 9 8 7 6 5 4 3 2 1

WALES

ENGLAND

King's Lynn   Norwich

Forest
of Arden   Coventry   Bury
                         St.Edmunds   Stovenham
Warwick   Cambridge   Cry Ashbourne
        Worcester   Banbury   Ipswich
Hereford   Colchester
            Oxford   Chelmsford
            Abingdon   London
                         River Thames
    Bristol   Dover

The Voyage of The Merchant of Orwell

the JOURNEY of
JOSLIN de LAY   Cherbourg

                    The
                  Castle at   La Cotentin
                  Treauville

                              FRANCE

*The Joslin de Lay Mysteries
are written in memory of
Tony Gibbs (1937–1966)
of Falmouth, Jesus College, Cambridge
and Langwith College, York,
who loved the Middle Ages
and would have been one of the greatest of
scholars and writers about them.*

A choking blanket of darkness smothered the girl. The worst terror of all had come. It had been her nightmare for as long as she could remember and now she was living through it. Screams and howls from killers and the ones they killed still echoed in her head. But they were nothing beside what she had been forced to watch.

She crouched on a rough, earthen floor. Cold rebounded from thick stone walls. She had been hurled against them hard and brutally. Now the bruises throbbed and pain sang in her ears. Blood trickled down her forehead.

But the men had left her alone, for a moment of blessed respite and peace. She tried to piece together what had happened. Where was her protector, who should have guarded her from these evils which had come from the awful world beyond the gates?

She knew well where he was. She'd seen what they did to him, right in front of her eyes. Strong arms held her so she was forced to watch. Her screams poured out from deep in her throat and rolled round that deep enclosed place. Her tormentors laughed.

There was no comfort left, no hope in all the world. She tried to pray, but she knew no words could leave this foul pit. She tried thinking of better things. Her human protector was beyond recall now, but he had not been the only rock she could depend on. There was something else, something that she loved more than any human being. If she thought about it hard enough she might see it, shining with a lustre only God could give. It might be a way through for her prayers.

She pummelled her head with her fists as she tried to conjure up the noble face, far-seeing eyes and folded wings of her Angel. But she couldn't. Her heart's desire had been taken away long ago and she did not know where it was. She had reached the end. Only death was left.

As if her tormentors read her thoughts, she sensed someone next to her in the pit. Had her time come? She heard tinder lit. In the tiny, flickering light a man's cruel face showed. The light went out again. The man's voice rasped in the darkness.

"Where is it?" He meant her heart's desire.

"I don't know. How I wish I did."

"You do know. Don't lie." Thwack! A gauntleted hand struck her left temple hard and jerked her head back.

"I don't. I don't."

There was silence. Then she heard firm feet stepping upwards and away, sure in spite of the darkness.

He would be back. Next time he would do worse. Her death was not far away, as terrible as the death she had just been made to watch.

She wouldn't wait for him to return. They thought

2

her woman's weakness would make her stay there, trembling and useless. But though she trembled, she was not useless. If she stilled her panic she could make her mind work clearly.

She took a deep breath. Did they know the way out, which was secret, except to her and – ? She bit back a sob. Could she find it in the dark? Would they hear her?

It didn't matter. If she was to die tonight, it would be bravely.

Cautiously she stood up. Though every muscle shrieked, she found she could move. She felt her way to stone steps and crept up to them. She stopped on the floor above. She heard voices. If these voices came from the next floor she was finished. She must take the chance.

She climbed the next steps and stood upright on a stone floor. Enough moonlight filtered in through arrow slits to give good bearings. Nobody was here. She breathed a prayer of thanks. She knelt and felt her way round the floor. Yes, here was the flagstone. She ran her fingers round it until she came to a little groove she could grip. Did she still have strength to lift it?

She strained and strained. The voices came no nearer.

At last the stone shifted. High enough to crawl underneath and let her feet tentatively down. Ah, they reached a comforting, strong floor. She let herself down completely. Gently, she replaced the flagstone above her head. She stopped dead still for a moment and regained her breath back. Then she inched slowly through darkness which now seemed friendly, along a narrow passageway which would take her to freedom.

At the end, she walked down more steps, opened a little door and scrambled through. She was in a proper room. Now he could see the golden image of the angel, her heart's desire, shining in the darkness to tell her that she had succeeded. But this image was real. In happier days she had sewn it herself on the tapestry which still hung there. Windows let in a little moonlight. What she saw nearly made her howl with grief because this room would never be lived in again. But she bit the cry back. She could get through a window easily enough. When she was a small girl she had often done it in play with her brothers.

Outside, the night air was like strong liquor. For a moment she stood and drank it in. But she had to be away. Moving like a shadow she glided through bushes and under trees until she reached the road outside. Now she sobbed aloud, with grief and relief together.

But she wasn't safe, was she? She would never be safe until she was protected by God's mighty power.

As if God spoke, she knew that there was such a place, that it was close by and that she could soon be there. Fully resolved now, she set out on her way.

Four years passed. Now Joslin de Lay and Crispin Thurn, minstrels both, were two days out of Coventry. June and high summer were here. Their horses walked along a westward track: Crispin's dark brown pony and Joslin's piebald, Herry, a long way from his old stables in London. They had travelled through the Forest of Arden and stayed for a night with friends who had done them great service, and now they had come to rolling, open country where wide rivers flowed, placid cattle grazed, crops grew well, and red soil hinted at plenty. Faintly purple hills smudged the western horizon. Joslin felt a thrill in his heart. Just beyond those hills was Wales and the end of his long journey. Nearly ten months had passed since that last night in France, when his father was murdered and he had fled to England.

"*North for Wales,*" his dying father had said as he lay on the deck of the *Merchant of Orwell*. "*And look for the blessed St Ursu. . .*" His eyes closed, but he rallied enough to give Joslin his belt and locket. "*Wear them always. There is only one key . . . and it belongs to your mother. . .*"

Then he died, and Joslin had carried on the quest ever since. "*Follow the sun and sing your way to Wales,*" said John Hammond, master of the *Merchant of Orwell*. So Joslin had, through danger, murder, hatred and friendship – even love. Yet through his dreams – and, did he but know it, dogging his footsteps – moved one he had seen during those last days in the Count's castle in France. A man with a sallow, pock-marked face and twisted mouth paced inexorably after him, just out of sight. Whatever final reckoning Joslin would meet beyond those mountains, this man was bringing part of it with him.

On the third day they came to Worcester. They found a good tavern close by, touched by a long evening shadow cast by the cathedral. Their horses were well watered, fed and stabled. Joslin and Crispin ate and drank and Joslin felt more at peace than he had for months.

Until Crispin ruined it. "Joslin," he said, "you and I have known each other for over a month now. That's a long time when you're on the move and sharing danger."

Joslin couldn't deny it. Crispin had saved his life

once, and in Coventry, Joslin had saved Crispin's. They had faced terror and escaped through their own wits. Yes, they knew each other well enough.

"So would you say you saw me as a friend?" Crispin continued.

"Of course I would," said Joslin. "And a good one."

"Then you must decide tonight," said Crispin. "Do we go on together or do we part here?"

"Why should we part?" cried Joslin. "You aren't going back to Coventry already?"

Before they left Coventry, Crispin had met Eleanor, the apothecary's daughter. They had fallen in love, but Crispin had said he would only go back when his business on the Welsh Marches was finished and he had something worth offering to a bride.

"No," Crispin replied. "What I said stands. I return when I'm ready. But now I turn south, to Hereford. You may not want that. Your way lies west."

"I don't know. You must give me time."

"But time's what we don't have. I leave early tomorrow for Hereford."

Joslin didn't answer.

"It would be a sorrow for me to go on alone now," said Crispin.

Still Joslin said nothing.

"But that's not fair of me," said Crispin. "I've got my quest to finish and you have yours, which means even more because you've left your own country to follow it. My concerns don't have to be yours."

"I know," said Joslin. "But. . ."

Crispin didn't let him finish the sentence. "Wait there," he said.

He got up off the bench and spoke to the landlord. Once he turned round and pointed at Joslin. The landlord listened, smiled, then nodded. Whatever Crispin had said was to his liking. It didn't take much for Joslin to know what it was.

Crispin came back. "Well, whether this is the last evening for which we're companions or not, it will be one to remember," he said.

"Don't tell me," Joslin answered. "We'll sing to them, won't we?"

"We certainly will. We're in a well set-up city – and a good tavern. We'll do well. We might need to. There won't be many more chances."

Joslin was well satisfied. Minstrelsy was what he did best.

"What shall you sing?" asked Crispin.

"I don't know. 'Sir Orfeo', perhaps. And 'The Tournament of Tottenham'. Those two together should give them a sigh and a laugh. What about you?"

Crispin grinned. "Wait and see," he said.

"You don't have to tell me," Joslin answered. "It's what you'll only give to audiences who deserve it. It's what you'll only play when the time is right. It's the song which holds the key to your own story. And if I hear it again, it may help me make up my mind whether or not to come with you tomorrow."

"That's right," said Crispin. "Tonight, Joslin, I shall sing the story of Gamelyn again."

That same night, as songs were sung in Worcester, strange things happened in Hereford.

In St Ethelbert's Cathedral, the masons' long day was finished, the last stone chipped, the last mortar mixed. Night had descended. Moonlight entered through the many-coloured windows. The high roof, with complicated patterns of stone arches meeting after dizzying journeys from the floor, was in darkness. No priest knelt before the high altar or in any chapel, no pilgrim muttered round St Thomas Cantilupe's shrine or stood before the Mappa Mundi imagining far-off, wondrous lands.

Yet the silence was not absolute, the vast church not deserted. Two figures had crept up the nave to the crossing in front of the choir and the high altar, separating them from the wide nave and the transepts on either side. The nave was where the ordinary folk congregated: in the transepts were side altars. Both figures wore cloaks, blacker even than the darkness they crept through. The first was tall and strong underneath that cloak. The other was smaller, slighter.

At each corner of the crossing, huge wooden baulks stretched up to the high roof. Round them was scaffolding. Together, they supported columns thicker than oak tree trunks but still not safe on their foundations. Resting on top of the baulks, where new arches were being put in place and mortared, was shuttering to keep the mortar in place until it dried.

The two who had moved so secretly up the nave came to the foot of a ladder. Its rungs stretched unnervingly upwards, insubstantial threads, to where it rested against a platform built into the scaffolding. But this ladder was only the first stage of the climb to where the new tower was being built. Years before, the plague had taken masons and money away. Just when Hereford thought it was recovering, the plague had come again, terrible as before, and taken yet more. This tower was left unfinished. Now, a generation with new wealth was able to complete the work. Then came a new disaster. The arches and columns which the Normans had put in place three hundred years before had slipped in their foundations. They had to be rebuilt, or this great cathedral of St Ethelbert would come crashing to the ground. Another reason for work to start urgently.

"The angel," said the first figure, in a whisper. "You said you want above all things to see the angel. Let me take you to see him."

The companion, who seemed to be a newcomer, answered, "Yes. Please do. I must see him."

"You go ahead," said the first. "I'll watch over you. You'll not fall."

The first seemed confident, the other frightened, though anxious to start this perilous climb. The two scaled the ladder, the one following a little after the other. The ladder's shafts bent and the rungs creaked under their weight: the spidery contraption seemed too weak to bear them both. The newcomer would not look down: this would mean blinding fear, hands suddenly nerveless and a helpless plunge to certain death. Sometimes, though, the urge to slow, stop, just cling on, was overpowering.

"Keep going," said the follower. "Don't look down. I'm here."

To the newcomer, the climb seemed endless. But it would be worth it if the tower were crowned with an exquisite carved golden angel. Except, of course, for the masons who had put him up, nobody knew that angel was here: it was a privilege to be told by one who knew so much. To see the beautiful object – to see him, what's more, by moonlight – was too great a spur to those hesitant feet.

The two climbers stepped off the frail wooden ladder and stood on the platform laid in the scaffolding. "We're halfway up the tower," said the first. "Here's another ladder to go up." This was easier. At least the ladder was shorter and enclosed within the scaffolding framework. At last their feet stood on stone. The newcomer scrambled to the welcome floor, stood, swayed, nearly fell backwards. But it would be a sad end to the expedition to be dashed to pieces far below.

"Where now?" asked the newcomer.

"Onward. Upward," said the other. "Yet another ladder."

Now the embrace of solid tower walls oppressed the newcomer with its darkness. "Why couldn't we climb up on the outside? There's scaffolding round the tower walls, with good walkways and more light."

"Of course we couldn't," replied the other. "We might be seen. You wouldn't risk that, would you? Do you want your superiors to know you'd been here at night, climbing a tower you have no business to?"

The newcomer said, "Anything is worth it, to see the golden angel shining in darkness and spreading goodness and beauty." But it was true. For the superiors to find out would be a sort of death in itself.

"We can feel our way upwards from here. It's safe enough. I know what I'm doing. I'm here to stop you falling."

Another ladder. "Not far to go," said the other. "One more ladder."

Now the newcomer could see night sky and twinkling stars and felt happier. There would not be much to stand on at the top, but the angel would be there. Just to see him – oh, just to *see* him.

The newcomer tentatively stepped off the ladder, snatched at the unfinished wall for support, looked round – *and saw no angel.* "Where is he? I can't see him."

The other left the ladder with perfect confidence and balance. "He is where angels always should be. Come out with me on to the scaffolding. You'll see better from there."

The newcomer stepped through a gap where a new wall would be built, avoiding blocks of dressed stone left ready for the next morning.

But something was still not right. "What do you mean?" said the newcomer. "I see no golden angel."

"You will in a moment. As good as that angel you have seen already. Tell me where it is now."

The newcomer cried aloud. "Only once have I seen an angel. Then he was taken away from me and never returned, except to my dreams. I wish I could have seen him every day for ever. But I didn't."

"You're lying to me," said the first.

"I swear I'm not, on the holy name of Jesus. I never knew what happened to him."

The patience of the other snapped: the sound of its snapping could be almost heard, like a taut harp string suddenly cut. "Then you're no use to me or to the world. Go where you'll see all the angels you want."

Hands with a strength beyond thought seized the small, light body. The newcomer gasped as the face under the other's hood was suddenly plain in the moonlight after all these years. "No, you can't be. . ." the newcomer cried. The cry was cut short, however, as the frail body was heaved over the side of the scaffolding. The cry turned into a last gasp, not of surprise but of supreme sadness because, after all, it had come to this. The murderer watched the body's almost graceful progress until it reached the roof of the nave. There, it teetered on the edge, nearly lodged in the guttering, then fell further like a monstrous bird shot with an arrow. It hit the ground below and spread out, very still, sprawling as if its arms and legs were carefully placed in some strange display. In the grey moonlight, its robe showed black against the stony ground, almost like the wings of an angel of death.

"Useless then, useless now," the murderer said, then stepped back inside the tower and felt a careful way down to the foot of the ladder.

Arthur Rawle, the bishop's chaplain, was a young priest who hoped for great things. He was just down from the University at Oxford and marked out for an important life in the Church. Not for him the cares of a humble parish priest: he lodged in a room in the bishop's place within the cathedral precincts. One day he would be a bishop himself. Meanwhile, it was enough to be in this beautiful city of Hereford, to pray and say Mass in such a wonderful cathedral as St Ethelbert. A fortunate chance for one so new to the priesthood. His life seemed perfect already. This was how it should carry on.

It was not always so. When he was a child strange things had sometimes happened to him at night. He had terrible dreams. He was told that he was seen walking abroad when he should have slept. He was chastised and a watch kept on him. But still, sometimes he rose as he slept and paced unseeing while his parents feared to stop him. At last, they brought a priest who muttered prayers, sprinkled him with holy water, asked for God's blessing and then commanded whatever devil was inside him to go at once. Since then his nights had been untroubled with dreams or nightmares. Until this one.

When he opened his eyes, hours too early on that bright June morning, he knew he had broken out of a nightmare. This terrible dream was so filled with horrors that his sudden waking left him trembling. He remembered nothing of what he went through, except an echoing fear of nameless things. Had he gone back to his childhood and risen from his bed while he was still sleeping? What had he done in those lost, dark hours?

Fully awake, he cried vain prayers for this awful cloud to leave. But it stayed stubbornly low. So he rose early. To take his mind off his terror, he went out of the palace to visit a sick cathedral warden who lived in Capuchin Lane on the north side of St Ethelbert's. When he left the old man, he cut across the green to a side entrance in the north transept under the central tower. He walked in the huge morning shadow cast by tower and nave.

He was to say the first Mass of the day. A mere young chaplain saying Mass in the cathedral? This was a measure of the trust Giles Longland, the bishop, put in him. He should be so happy. But his heart was troubled and his mind full of foreboding.

Suddenly, he stopped. What was that black shape on the ground under the scaffolding which ringed the central tower? Something about its shape, like a gigantic stranded bat, made him shudder. At first he wanted to turn his eyes away, pretend he had not seen it, pass by on the other side. But that was not what a priest should do. He changed direction, curious, apprehensive, then, ten paces away, he was seized with revulsion which sent foul-tasting bile into his mouth.

He saw a body, broken and bleeding. Without thinking, he looked up. It must have fallen from the scaffolding round the tower. He took a deep breath and went nearer.

That bruised, staring face. Did he know it? It was a woman's face. Her white hair was matted with blood from her broken head, though her face was young. And those black robes spread out like a ruined fan – a nun's habit.

He swallowed. This was impossible. Why should a nun be here, alive or dead, in the early morning when the curfew at St Katherine's nunnery, three miles out of the city, was so strict? How could a nun have fallen from the tower?

The prioress must be told, and soon. But first, the bishop must hear. Thankful that he could shrug the cares of at least this horror off on to someone else, he turned on his heel and ran as fast as he could, shaking, white-faced, into the cathedral.

The previous evening, when the landlord announced that there would be good entertainment, the citizens of Worcester crowded to the tavern as word spread of two visiting minstrels.

"You first," muttered Crispin. "We'll each do one song alternately."

Joslin sang "Sir Orfeo". This ballad had served him well lately and had become his favourite. Orfeo's queen, Heurodys, was spirited away to Faeryland. Orfeo, with only his harp and his music, went looking for her, found his way to the throne of the Faery King and played so beautifully that even that fearsome

15

creature was won over. Heurodys, released, came out of Faeryland with Orfeo, back to their old happy life and many long years of contentment. Joslin thought about his own quest. Would it have the same happy ending? Once, years ago, a wandering scholar had come to the castle at Treauville and told Guillaume and Joslin that, in times long past, Orfeo's story as the ancients knew it had no happy ending but a lifetime of loneliness for Orfeo with nothing but music to live for. Perhaps his own ending would be the same.

When "Orfeo" was over, Crispin stepped forward. His drum was slung over his shoulder. He held his flute in his hand.

"I shall sing you the story of Gamelyn," he said. "It's a long tale. But I'll stop between each part and give you a rest. And me as well. I'll call you to order each time I restart." Joslin smiled. He'd heard Crispin say that before.

Crispin gave a roll on the drums and a fanfare on the flute. Then his deep voice cut through the air and everyone was quiet.

"*Now, shut up and listen and get this right.*"

So on went the story, about how old Sir John left his lands equally to his eldest son John, the second son Otis and Gamelyn, the youngest. But John cheated Gamelyn out of his share and treated him like a slave.

Gamelyn beat the local wrestling champion and brought all the folk round about on to his side. But when John locked him out for ever, he went away into the forest, became the outlaw king and later led his men into the city where John was sheriff. There they captured him and hanged him, along with all his cheating friends. So Gamelyn took possession of his rightful inheritance, married, and lived long and happily until God called them both to: ". . . *that great joy on high.*"

Well, Joslin had made most of this story fit with Crispin – the forest, the outlaws, becoming the outlaw king, even the wrestling match. And now, with Eleanor, he could even look forward to ". . . *that great joy on high.*" Which he certainly couldn't before, and might not still, if he didn't sort his mysterious business in the Welsh Marches out properly.

The song of Gamelyn ended and the people of Worcester were well pleased with it. Even so, one man in the crowd looked hard at Crispin, then quietly stole out of the tavern.

He was certain. This was the one he remembered and had been told to look for. After all these years, Crispin was very near.

The man went into the stable and took out his horse. Now he had to ride fast through the night. After all, he reasoned, if Crispin were so near his old home after so long an absence, he wouldn't waste any more time. He'd be up at first light and on his way as soon as he could.

The man turned out of the inn yard and set off on the Hereford road. As he rode, he calculated. Crispin would move fast – though not as fast as *he* now would to bring back this news. Crispin might be near Hereford by late morning, early afternoon, no later.

What about that minstrel singing with him? A chance companion, or a new associate? Hard to say. Whatever, they should look out for either a single horseman or a pair tomorrow, who would be near home when the sun was about at its highest. Easy enough. The road from Worcester to Hereford was not as busy as it used to be in the days before the plague.

He sniggered to himself. The person he was taking this news to would make sure Crispin's visit was violent and very short.

In the tavern, the evening wore on. Joslin gave them "The Tournament of Tottenham", which was always good for a laugh. Then it was Crispin's turn. "One more," he said. "And then you'll have to sing for yourselves. You don't realize what thirsty work this is."

"What will it be?" people shouted.

"I'll sing 'Sir Gawain and the Carl of Carlisle'," Crispin answered. Joslin remembered this from their last night in Coventry. Sometimes it was funny, sometimes bloodthirsty. He'd liked it and wanted to learn it. Without pausing, Crispin was away:

> "I'll tell you a tale, not too long, not too short,
> That you've not heard before, about King Arthur's court
> And one particular knight.
> This knight was as gentle as a maiden fair,
> But one sign of trouble and he'd be there
> Spoiling for a fight.
> 'Who is he?' you ask. Why, Sir Gawain, of course.
> In all Britain, no better knight ever rode horse."

On and on he sang, pausing now and again for deep draughts of beer, until the Carl of Carlisle's last triumphant shout:

> "'And EVERYTHING'S GOING TO BE GREAT!'"

Then, before the crowd could make a sound, he was off again.

"Well, that's my song, that's my story –
Not too long and not too gory:
And if you stayed awake through this
Then may you be brought to eternal bliss."

Then came his last word, two long notes, loud, half-mocking, half-thankful. *"A-MEN."*

All the folk were on their feet, stamping, cheering, yelling for more. "Not from me. I'm near dead with the effort," said Crispin.

"What about your friend, then?" shouted a voice. "How can I follow that?" Joslin answered. Besides, he'd had enough for one evening. He needed quiet now to make a big decision.

But the folk didn't seem to mind. The money was pouring into Joslin's open pannier. Perhaps they couldn't listen any more, either.

Well to the west by now, the horse ridden by the man who had slipped out of the tavern was cantering easily along a road which, even though dark and lonely, held no terrors for him.

He wasn't as happy now as he was when he started out. "Will I be thanked for my news?" he said to himself.

He couldn't answer his own question. He had his doubts. He shivered at the thought of what might happen to him if he wasn't.

The tavern was emptying. Joslin and Crispin were dividing the money. Joslin was still making up his mind about what to do tomorrow. He knew that Crispin was fast approaching whatever lay in store for his quest – and if it was like the song he had just sung, it might be dangerous, with blood flowing. Or it might be gentle, pleasant and welcoming. Who could tell?

How much did he want to be part of it? By now, Crispin was a true friend. In the last weeks they had rescued each other in turn, so on that score honour was even. But there was more to it. Joslin couldn't forget how Crispin looked at Eleanor in the apothecary's in Coventry. The man was so close to his heart's desire. Joslin wanted so much for him to go back in triumph to claim Eleanor.

"Finished?" said Crispin. "Are you satisfied? Is the money fair?"

"Yes, it's fair," Joslin answered. Then, quickly, so he couldn't hesitate again, he said. "Crispin, I'm coming with you to Hereford."

Crispin put a hand on Joslin's shoulder, stood back to arm's length and looked steadily at him. "Thank you," he said. "You can't know how pleased that makes me."

Much had happened round the cathedral since Arthur found the body. As he entered late, the bishop, Giles Longland, the dean, Ivo de Trellick, and several canons were in the sacristy. All these grave clerics looked at him disapprovingly. Giles Longland never said the first Mass: he believed it was his time for meditation and the dean and chapter agreed. Arthur unworthily wondered if making him do it was really so they could give themselves time to wake up properly. This morning though, Arthur kept garbling the familiar words and Giles Longland shot him glances, at first enquiring, then furious. Arthur dreaded the coming interview. As he came to the "Agnus Dei" his mind wandered. Might the bishop see the black pit in his mind – or know about that shattered body already?

The second was doubtful. That morning, Arthur had approached the cathedral from the dying churchwarden's house in Capuchin Lane on the north side. Giles Longland's palace was on the south, where the morning sun shone. So were the lodgings of the dean and canons. The folk came to mass through the west door. Nobody could possibly have seen the dead nun. Even the lean-to shack, dignified with the name of mason's lodge, was on the sunny side, out of sight. The masons wouldn't start work until the day's first Mass was over. So they wouldn't have seen it, either.

Arthur's heart sank further. The burden of telling about the appalling discovery was his alone.

The Mass was over quicker than usual. "Ita missa est," Arthur gabbled and rushed for the sacristy. Giles Longland followed slowly, fury mottling his large face. But before he could speak, Arthur stuttered, "My Lord. You must see. . ."

"What am I to see?" said the bishop in a dangerously quiet voice. "Is it your irreverent blasphemy this morning, for which I should send you packing far away? I've seen that already. It has disgusted me and offended God. I had high hopes of you, Arthur. I see I was wrong."

"My lord, please wait," said Arthur. "The true blasphemy lies outside." In spite of his panic, he was proud of that remark. "You must see it, before masons and other common people do."

Giles looked at him narrowly. "No young priest would dare speak to his bishop of blasphemy unless a devil had entered his soul," he said. Arthur shivered at those words. The bishop knew about his dream: *of course* he knew.

"Unless, for some reason, he meant it," Giles continued. "For the moment I shall presume you meant it. Lead me to this new blasphemy." He turned to the others. "There is no call for you to come. If I need you, you'll be there soon enough."

Every step of the way, Arthur feared Giles knew

what festered in his mind, that a devil was in his soul and there was no dead body there. When they reached the tower, he was ashamed to feel glad that the corpse still lay untouched.

Giles Longland gasped slightly, then cleared his throat to hide such weakness. But Arthur noticed and felt relieved. Giles was, after all, a man as others were. Giles bent down and gingerly touched the face. "She is cold," he said. "But there is no decay yet. She died during the night."

To anyone else, Arthur would have said, "Of course she did, you old fool. She wasn't here yesterday, was she?" To his bishop, he gravely replied, "I believe you must be right, my lord."

"Fetch the dean," said Giles.

Arthur thankfully left him. He was trembling with dark imaginings. Finding this body had followed his nightmare as day follows night and he was giddy with what it might mean. Ivo de Trellick was shuffling past the bishop's palace. He turned at once when Arthur gasped, "The bishop wants you."

When Ivo saw what the body wore, he said, "We must bring the prioress of St Katherine's nunnery here. She should be the first to see her sister."

"I agree," said Giles. "I shall return to the palace. I shall send a messenger to the nunnery. Meanwhile, Arthur, you will stand guard by this poor woman. Let nobody come near."

Giles was gone before Arthur drew breath, walking fast without quite breaking into an unseemly trot. Ivo followed three paces behind. His job was to ride the three miles to St Katherine's. Giles's, no doubt, was to kneel in prayer in his palace.

Left alone, Arthur was back in his nightmare. A

devil was at work here. Perhaps this nun was not dead. How could he bear to see the dead walk again, eyes open, fixed and staring, slack mouth gibbering, accusing fingers pointing?

He made himself look at the body. No, she was certainly dead. He felt a strange guilt. Was *that* what his dream was about? Could *he* have hurled the poor nun to her death as he thought he was sleeping, and forgotten because the devil did not want him to remember?

Arthur pulled himself together. Ever since he could remember he had felt guilty for what others had done. "The weight of other people's confessions on your shoulders will kill you when you're a priest, my boy," his father once said and, deep down, Arthur knew how true that was. He must stop feeling this, or he would not last five years. But now a shroud of doubt smothered him – that he *really was guilty*.

The sun had moved a long way round the sky, before Agatha, prioress of St Katherine's Nunnery, arrived with Giles Longland and Ivo de Trellick. She was tall and austere. The look on her square, strong face struck fear into Arthur's heart. She looked sourly at him. Then she inclined her head towards the dead nun.

"Christina," she said at once. "A good woman and one of our own. We will take her and see to her burial."

"I fear you can't," said Ivo. "Not yet. It grieves me to say it, but the civil powers must see her corpse and start their enquiries. We must fetch Edwin Pendock, the Justice of the Peace and coroner."

"I repeat, she is one of our own," Agatha replied firmly. "You can tell Edwin Pendock what happened and he will believe you. I will not leave her poor remains for idle rough men to stare at and snigger over. We have a priest of our own and he will perform all the rites necessary."

In spite of his terrors, Arthur watched the two, fascinated. This was a battle of wills. The dean would win, of course – he was the dean and a man and spoke with the bishop's full power. Beside him, what was a mere woman, however godly and severe, whatever her title? So when Giles Longland motioned Ivo to keep quiet and said, "Very well. Have her taken to your nunnery and be disposed of as is proper," Arthur was surprised. When it came to a battle of wills, Sister Agatha was stronger than he thought.

"The masons have a cart," said Ivo. He turned to Arthur. "Find Hubert Fennel, the master mason. He must pick three men who will keep quiet and not blab. They're to be here with a cart and cloths. Tell him they will be gone some hours."

"Do as he says," said Giles.

"My lord," said Arthur obediently.

"Tell Hubert you'll be going with them," said Ivo. "Say also that you'll be coming straight back, so neither a doleful errand nor a good working day will be polluted by time lost in taverns on the way."

"At once, Arthur," said Giles.

"My lord," Arthur repeated, sounding obedient but feeling less so.

"See it done," said Giles Longland.

"My lord," said Arthur for a third time, failing to hide his horror at being in this dead nun's company for hours yet.

It wasn't making sure his workmen didn't keep

sloping off to the tavern which upset Hubert Fennel's working day. No, first it was anger at finding that his tool store had been disturbed in the night. Every working day, the long ladder was placed in the crossing so masons could reach the top of the arch and climb further up the scaffolding. There was as much work to be done inside as outside. The dean didn't like it – but the dean wasn't master mason and if this work was to be finished, then Hubert insisted on having his way. Anyway, the ladder and scaffolding were fenced off so they got in nobody's way. No workman would dream of climbing it while a Mass was on, so what could Ivo de Trellick have to complain about? Every night, the long ladder was locked in the tool store by the masons' lodge. Last night, though, it was not where Hubert knew they had put it back. Only two handspans from its proper place – but *wrong*. Hubert hated things which were wrong, no matter by how little.

The watchman's name was Ulf. He was small, and stunted. Only fit, thought Hubert, for sitting awake all night and watching for intruders. Though Hubert didn't know what Ulf would do if one came. Still, they had to look after him. His mother died in the plague and his father, a good journeyman carpenter and builder, had been found murdered in Grope Lane five years before and the killer was never caught. If Hubert had his way, soldiers would guard the store, but Ivo said God surrounded it with power enough to keep evil men away. Even Ulf being there was a small victory for Hubert.

Ulf blinked rapidly as Hubert asked what had happened last night. "No, master," he gabbled. "Nobody came to the store. I was in my place all night. I never closed my eyes. I wouldn't, master, not for the world."

"God help us, man, the ladder went!" shouted Hubert.

A catalogue of expressions crossed Ulf's face – fear, horror, shiftiness. Guilt didn't seem one of them. Then he mumbled, "I must have slept through it."

"I should have you put in the stocks for a raving idiot," shouted Hubert.

"Be merciful," said Giles. "The man is on sacred ground and he deserves another chance to make good."

Hubert muttered to himself, then said aloud, "Very well. But I'll have my eye on you, young Ulf." The inconvenience of the dead nun under the tower was a much greater worry than any half-daft watchman. Nuns had nothing to do with him, nor he with them. But what upset him most were needless, useless questions from Edwin Pendock, Justice of the Peace and coroner, bombarding his ears. No, he had not slipped out at night, pushed that poor nun up a tower and thrown her off the scaffolding. He was a master mason, wasn't he? He'd worked hard to get where he was and he wasn't going to lose it all by hurling useless nuns to their deaths from this great work, the summit of his ambitions. And what would any of his men want to do such a thing for?

"Some men think sport with a woman forbidden to them's the best sport of all," said Edwin Pendock.

"Not if you've thrown her off the highest tower in the county first, it's not," Hubert replied.

The coroner said nothing, as if there was no answer to that. He spent half the day interrogating the other masons until he was sure he had no reason to suspect any of them. Ulf was certainly not strong enough to tip even a small nun over the top. No, it was clear what happened. Ulf had dozed off, then woken up. In that time, an intruder came in, took the key, removed the ladder, did the job, put it back, though not quite in the right place, replaced the key and crept off.

Morning was half gone before the questioning was done. Hubert Fennel sighed with relief. Then Edwin asked another question. "Who found the body?"

"Well, none of us, if that's what you're thinking," said Hubert. "She'd been carted off before we started work. It was some priest. He's gone with the body, Sister Agatha and our cart."

"A priest and a prioress pushing a cart?" Edwin didn't believe this.

"No. I sent Robin Greylad, Abel Simpkin and Will Cater with them."

"Three more masons?"

Hubert sighed, He would be stuck with this man until they came back. "They know nothing. They couldn't kill a fly, let alone a nun," he said wearily.

Sister Agatha had said they would be away for some hours and she was right. The sun was bright and the day was getting hotter. The little procession trundled away from the cathedral, along Mill Lane, across Little Packers Lane, cutting through into St Peter's Street, up Grope Lane past the Market, then into the wide Bye Street, through Bysters Gate and out on to the road to Bromyard leading north-east.

Robin, Abel and Will bent to the shafts. Agatha rode on, eyes fixed on a point ahead, her pony buck-ling slightly under her weight. Arthur shuffled behind, hands clasped, muttering prayers for the dead. In the city, people stood aside and crossed themselves. Once on the open road, they were on their own. For three miles they trudged. The sun shone down. The masons became hotter and thirstier. Arthur hoped there would be no nonsense about going into taverns on the way home.

When they reached the nunnery, nuns young and old watched curiously from gardens and windows. Arthur heard quiet crying and this nameless guilt rose again, that he could be the cause. Agatha led the men into a courtyard, then disappeared into the prioress's room. They waited outside, watched by tearstained faces. Arthur felt more and more awkward.

When Agatha reappeared, she was with an older nun. Arthur knew her to be the manciple, who looked after the day-to-day running of the nunnery. The manciple motioned the masons to lift the body and carry it into the chapel. Trestles were ready: Christina was laid on top and covered with more seemly cloths than Hubert had provided.

Though the words stuck to the roof of his mouth, Arthur said more prayers to receive Christina into the chapel and speed her soul onwards. Agatha knelt and muttered to herself: Arthur dared not move until she rose. This seemed a long time. Finally, she unwound her great height and stood towering over him.

"You can go now," she said. "All will be done properly: have no fear about that. We have our own priest who will bury her."

Leaving St Katherine's seemed a release from prison. The masons wheeled the cart light-heartedly: Arthur followed. Outside the nunnery the road bent to the left. The cathedral tower showed clear from all of three miles away. As the masons pushed the cart on to the road, Will said, "Master Hubert won't mind if we drop into a tavern."

"But the Church will," said Arthur. "The bishop forbids it. I am charged to bring you back."

Will muttered to himself. Arthur sensed the masons were no longer so well disposed towards him.

Outside the entrance to the grounds of St Katherine's, and almost opposite the way in to a manor house, was a thicket of rowan trees. Suddenly, Robin pointed at it. "Mother of God and all saints and angels, what's that?" he squealed.

The thin, close-packed tree trunks fought upwards for sunlight. What for a moment looked like a less successful tree in the striving mass could easily go unnoticed. Except for an arm lolling out where they could see it.

They stopped. The masons tore their eyes away from the sight and looked towards Arthur. His face was deathly pale. His heart was pounding and the dreadful fears swept down on him again.

"Will you look and tell us what it is, your grace?" said Abel.

He nearly said, "You mustn't call me 'your grace'. I'm not the bishop, only his chaplain." But now wasn't the time. He was the man of God and in the face of death everyone turned to him. If only they knew. Arthur took a deep breath and forced himself to go closer.

He found a man, dead. One tree was oddly shaped, with two trunks dividing just above the roots. The body was wedged standing between the two trunks of this tree. The man wore the tunic of an ordinary serf. His face was blotched, bloody and pulped as though he had fallen directly on to his face. It was hard to see any features on it at all. His broken limbs stuck out at grotesque angles like a doll a witch would pierce with pins to make her enemy scream in agony. Arthur had a strange feeling that if he had not found this man upright here, he would find him spread-eagled and broken on the ground after falling from a great height, as he had found Sister Christina.

There were hoofbeats behind them. Will looked up and turned round. "Who are you?" he said.

Two horsemen stood there. "Mother of God, what's that?" said one.

"A poor man evilly done to death," said Abel.

The other horseman spoke. "A fine welcome to Hereford this is," he said. "All the more reason for going straight past it."

"Who are you?" Will repeated.

"Two travellers on our way to Bristol," said the first. "And since we have no wish to be caught up in other people's travails, having plenty of our own, we'll bid you good day and leave you to your task. We certainly won't be lodging in Hereford for the night. We'll make another twenty miles before nightfall."

Then they were gone, in a canter, leaving a cloud of dust behind them.

Arthur was still looking at the body. He wanted to retch violently: in one day he had found two bodies done to death in terrible ways. The feeling that Death was at his own heels and reaching a bony hand to take him was too strong to keep down. The first one gave him guilt enough. But that was in his own cathedral, not a hundred paces from where he slept. He told himself he would have to sleepwalk at the speed of angels to have anything to do with this

That morning, the tavern was empty except for Joslin and Crispin putting money into their moneybelts. The landlord gave them a good breakfast, filled their tankards with ale and said, "Take as long as you like to drink it and welcome. If you want more, just ask. I'm right grateful to you both." Then he left.

"So you'll come with me," said Crispin. "Yet you don't know what you're letting yourself in for."

"I don't care," said Joslin. "I've been in England eight months now and nothing surprises me any more. Besides I want to see how things turn out for you."

"That's good," said Crispin appreciatively.

"Remember, I saw Eleanor in Coventry as well," said Joslin. "I want you two to be. . ."

"Not half as much as I do," Crispin quietly interrupted.

"So what's your story?" said Joslin.

"I thought you knew it," Crispin replied. "You've heard 'Gamelyn' often enough."

"I know," Joslin answered. "But. . ."

33

"Then you tell me," said Crispin.

"You're an infuriating man," Joslin said impatiently. "It's not as if 'Gamelyn' was made up just to tell your story. You told me you heard it in the forest and thought it seemed to apply to you."

"Every story applies to somebody," Crispin observed.

Joslin knew he'd get no further without doing some work himself. Not for the first time, he wouldn't get a straight story out of Crispin.

"All right," he said. "Let's see. Gamelyn was the youngest of three brothers. Old Sir John left them his land equally. John the eldest and Otis, the next, did all right. But John cheated Gamelyn out of his share. Is that what happened to you?"

"More or less," Crispin replied. "My father had lands north of Hereford. He wasn't a lord or knight. In fact, once he was a serf. But his old master, Sir Redvers, gave him his freedom and made him bailiff. After the plague, when Sir Redvers had lost his family and nearly all his bondmen, he gave half his land to my father. Well, my father was a good master and a good husbandman himself. He prospered. He built a fine house. He served his sheriff and king. He was respected by his betters – why, if he hadn't died, the king might have knighted him."

"And you had two elder brothers?" Joslin asked.

"One brother, older than me. Two sisters, one older than me, the other much younger. Luke was my brother's name." Crispin stopped. Joslin waited.

When he spoke again, his voice was fierce. "In all my life, nobody ever dared show me contempt. I've made sure of that." Joslin believed it. "Except one – the one I most wanted to think well of me." He looked away. "If you really want to know me, you have to know this."

"Why would he show you contempt?" asked Joslin.

Crispin picked up his flute and put his fingers in the holes as though he was going to play. Then he lowered it. "That's why," he said.

"Because you sang songs?" Joslin cried incredulously.

"Luke said singing should be left to women. Any man who sang and played was no better than a weak woman."

"Did your father think so, too?" asked Joslin.

"Not he," said Crispin. "He was proud that I was a good minstrel. He saw how bad things were between Luke and me. He said I should go away for a while, earn money, stand on my own feet, come back and show Luke I had more ways of making a living than from the land. 'Half a year,' he said. 'Then come back. If you do well, you'll find that half the land is yours when I die, to go with a talent your brother hasn't got, and which should not be hidden under a bushel.' Well, I did what he said. I journeyed through the shire and even into Wales. I stood on my own feet. I earned my keep and paid my way. After six months I came back twice the man I was when I left. But then. . ."

He stopped again. "Well?" said Joslin.

"My father was dead. Luke had it all. Our sisters were shut away in a top room, fated to stay there until Luke saw fit to let them out. He would only give them dowries to marry men of his choosing."

"How did your father die?" said Joslin, suddenly suspicious.

"I don't know," Crispin replied. "And nobody would tell me. The mere question made men turn pale and look away." He looked at Joslin's face. "Yes, I know what you're thinking. I think the same. Secret foul play was done to my father. I know it. And I mean to find out what it was."

"So what did you do?"

"I told Luke what I thought. I told him I'd find out and prove it. For answer, he set dogs on me and drove me out of the house and the whole domains. 'And never come back,' he shouted at me. 'This place is barred to you for ever.' What could I do? I left, vowing that one day I'd return. You know the rest of the story – how I went eastwards to Arden Forest and what happened to me there. After all those adventures, I heard news in Leicester from a traveller from the west. He told me there were rumours all over Hereford. Some said Luke was living alone, like a hermit. Others said he'd gone on a journey and hadn't come back. Something strange was happening in that house. I had to find out what it was. Besides, it was time I sought what was properly mine. So I started the journey home. You know what happened on that."

"What about your sisters all this time?" Joslin asked.

"That worries me, Joslin. I've heard nothing. They might be married. If Luke chose the man, I hope each can bear to be with whoever they've got."

There was something else. "I know your brother's name," said Joslin. "But what were your sisters called?"

"The elder was Margaret. We called her Madge."

"And the younger?"

"Christina," Crispin answered.

Christina was buried. Arthur and the masons had left with their empty cart. The nuns were at their daily tasks. The normal life of St Katherine's slowly came back.

When the burial was over, Agatha spent some hours in prayer. But she knew what she had to do. She would not sit here fretting. She knew Christina's story, or some of it, but she would tell nobody, not even Sister Freya. She would go where her suspicions took her.

Agatha's chestnut pony was called Daw. No one else possessed such a luxury except Freya, the manciple, with her spavined, knock-kneed nag. But Agatha insisted – a pony was not an indulgence. She often had to get to the city and deal with those obtuse men in the cathedral. Daw was looked after by Sister Joan, the oldest nun in St Katherine's. Apart from seeing to the mounts of occasional visitors, looking after Daw and Freya's horse was her only duty. But she lavished all her care and love on Daw. Every night, she slept in the straw near him. Agatha knew that one day they would find Joan dead there.

Agatha stood in the courtyard. "Joan," she called.

The old nun came out at once.

"Saddle up Daw and bring him to me," Agatha commanded. "I have important business outside. It concerns Christina."

Joan did as she was told. Soon, she led the pony out, helped the prioress on to his back and tightened up girths and harness. Then, she watched the pair as they slowly moved off. The sight of the bulky woman sitting on the tiny horse would have made anyone else laugh, but to Joan, Agatha was like a knight shining in black armour, mounted on a huge and snorting destrier, moving fearsomely into battle.

Until the four frightened men returned to the cathedral with an empty cart and doleful news, at least Hubert Fennel had got on with his work, even though three of his workforce were missing. Now he would still have to do without them, because Edwin Pendock insisted on seeing this new death at once and then having the corpse brought into the city.

"My lord," cried Arthur in anguish to the bishop. "Do I have to go?" Seeing that second body again would be worse than torments in hell.

Giles looked at him severely. "You do," he said.

Evening approached as the five retraced their steps. When they reached the rowan trees, Abel cried, "It's all right. He's been taken away." It seemed he was right. Where before an arm had dangled out over the road, now there was nothing.

Edwin almost burst out with fury at a wasted journey. But Robin was looking deeper into the trees. "Look, master," he cried quaveringly to Edwin. "See it there, like a poor creature trying to hide so the devil won't find him and take him away."

Robin was right. The body was tucked deeper into the thicket, so that only someone who knew it was there could possibly see it.

"Well, he didn't get there himself," said Will. "Somebody pushed him in. And we'll have to drag him out, the poor creature."

"It's only dead," Edwin replied. "So will you be when your Lord wants you. Dying is the least of our worries. When you've seen as many dead as I have. . ."

He ordered the three unwilling masons to extricate the body from the thicket and lay it on the cart. Arthur fell to his knees, and Edwin looked away. Not until the body was laid out did Edwin examine it.

"I don't know the man," he said. "Do any of you?"

The masons shook their heads. Robin spoke for them. "No, master," he said. "Yet the jaw has a set to it I've seen before."

Will laughed bitterly. "How can anyone look at those poor pulped features and think they know them?" he said.

"I say Robin's right," said Abel. "There's something about him that's known to me, but I can't tell you where I saw him."

"Well, wherever it is, it's not far away because you haven't been nowhere but Hereford," said Will.

"That's true," said Abel. "But I still can't say who it is."

Edwin Pendock bent and touched the head. Arthur remembered what he thought when he first saw it. "Is it possible that he was thrown from a great height, just as Sister Christina was?" he asked.

Edwin did not answer for some minutes. He felt the battered features and broken bones, manipulated the lifeless joints, examined the livid bruises and cuts, then stepped back and straightened up. "I believe you may be right," he said. "Yet this fall was later than Christina's. God's final rigor has not set in."

"Well, he never fell off our tower then," said Will. "Not unless Hubert and the bishop dragged him out and wedged him in while we were at the priory."

"Don't be daft," said Abel.

When Arthur had finished reprimanding Will for speaking so lightly of Giles Longland, Edwin said, "There are more places than one for a man to fall to his death." He bent again and looked at the battered face. "When did you find him?" he asked.

"When we came out of the nunnery," said Abel.

"Was the body there when you went in?"

The masons looked at each other. "That it weren't," said Will.

"That's right," said Robin.

Edwin turned to Arthur. "Was it?" he asked.

"No," said Arthur. "No, I'm sure it wasn't."

"Strange," said Edwin. "It was carefully placed there while you were at St Katherine's. That would be late morning. Why?" He bent down again. Then he said, "Are you sure his arm was showing before?"

"Yes, master," said Abel. "We wouldn't have seen him else."

"I can vouch for that," said Arthur.

"Strange. So someone moved him while you were away. Who? Why?" Edwin was deep in thought. "And did he fall to his death? What about that mangled face? Would a fall cause that? Perhaps someone set about his face with cudgels and staves after he was dead, so that nobody would ever recognize him."

"No," said Arthur, horrified. "No such evil as that. Not in the blessed and saintly city of Hereford."

"I fear you may have a rude awakening," Edwin murmured. "Ruder even than what has already happened to you today."

Arthur felt panic. Had this man of justice divined his secret?

Edwin was looking up at the sky. "We must go back now," he said. "Otherwise we'll still be on the road in the dark."

Abel covered the body in the shroud that had covered Christina. Then the little procession set off on its slow journey. Dusk was nearly falling by the time they came to Hereford. Outside the gates, two travellers on horseback overtook them. "Remember those horsemen this morning when we found the body?" said Robin. "I hope they're miles away from here by now."

"Horsemen? What horsemen?" demanded Edwin.

As they told him and Edwin wondered if there might be any connection, two new horsemen walked past slowly, making the sign of the cross when they saw the body, and entered Byster's Gate by the city wall ahead of them. Arthur quietly breathed thanks to them: some would show no respect. Edwin told the masons to stop at Byster's Gate. He spoke to the guard: then the body was laid out in an upper room. Arthur made sure everything was done properly, then he returned to the cathedral, said prayers with Giles – none of which, he felt, would work because his mind was not on them – and came back to his room as dusk was falling, to make ready for evening Mass in a side chapel.

His fears of Death as a bony traveller on a dusty road rose once more, and this time would not go away. He tried hard to shake off this figure patrolling his mind, but it stayed with him throughout his useless private prayers and still dogged him as he rose to go to the cathedral.

This was no good. These fears would drown him. He needed to talk to someone. But who? There was no way he could speak confidentially to the bishop. Giles would not begin to understand. Ivo de Trellick? That stern, dried up stickler for everything being just so? Never. Any other priest? He thought of them one by one and mentally crossed them out. Being at St Ethelbert's was wonderful – but it meant that he spent his life with old men.

Edwin Pendock? Not for a problem like this. If he could say something useful about the murders, then perhaps. But not about these ghosts in the mind. No, he needed someone his own age with the hopes and fears of youth. Arthur still had them and would, he hoped, never lose them, even though he had thrown in his lot with the priesthood. He must speak to someone who might also stay awake at night racked with fears and doubts, who might understand.

But who? He knew nobody in Hereford. Even if he did, no priest would dare confess weakness to an ordinary person. Why would anyone make confessions if they thought priests were as ordinary as they were?

Nobody in Hereford. But perhaps a stranger, somebody he didn't even know yet? He remembered the two travellers respectfully passing the cart with the body on it. They were young, one of them especially so. Now he recalled an alert, keen face which he somehow knew instinctively would sympathize and understand, framed in long dark hair which made him seem not from these parts. From the far west of Wales, perhaps? At any rate, their horses were loaded with panniers: they were certainly on a journey. Surely they must stop here, even if only for one night. Perhaps, if he really looked, he could find them.

He wiped the thought out. There was no hope. He'd never see that young one again. He was locked inside his own terrors with no way out.

Edwin Pendock was thinking about the second body wedged in the rowan trees. This man was well over thirty years old – not in his youth any more. There seemed nothing remarkable about him except the manner of his death. Might the young priest be right about him being thrown from a great height? The sight of Christina lying under the tower must be fixed in Arthur Rawle's mind for ever. But Christina had been left where she fell. If this man had died the same way, then someone had taken the trouble to carry him away from whatever high place he had fallen off to where sooner or later he would be found. Then he made the body easy to see by letting an arm dangle free, but afterwards seemed to think again and tried to conceal it. What sort of mad behaviour was that? How strange to kill a man and then say, "Look what I've done." How much stranger to say, "No, I'll hide him after all."

The more Edwin turned these things over in his mind, the more mystified he was. Any other time, he would have called on Luke Thurn whose manor and domains were opposite the nunnery, to see if he had anything to say. But was Luke there? Some rumours said that he had gone on a journey and nobody knew when he would return. Others said that he was there all the time, living like a hermit. Who could tell?

There was only one way to find out. He'd go there tomorrow. But now he was so tired. He would be glad when he could climb into his bed.

At the beginning of that long day, Joslin and Crispin had been still in Worcester, prepared to be away early. The panniers were packed, Herry and Cob saddled up. Joslin's father's locket was safe. He rattled it and pondered yet again on what the object inside was and whether it really did hide the answers to his own mysteries. Well, his journey wasn't far off its finish now. He might find the truth just over the mountains in the west, which he would cross when his business with Crispin was done in Hereford.

But then the landlord stopped them. "Gentlemen," he said. "Could you do me a favour? Your fame has spread to my patrons' wives and children. They're outside, hoping you'll give them a song before you go."

He was right. Outside, a crowd of women and children waited, eyes wide with hope. Impatience crossed Crispin's face: then he said, "No, I've spent so long on this journey, a few extra hours won't hurt me."

So they sang, singly and together, love songs for the women, short and happy songs for the children, hour after hour until time seemed not to matter. At last, Crispin stopped. "I'm sorry, ladies and youngsters," he said, "but we have a journey and cannot delay any more. We'd have reached our destination before the end of the morning and now we won't make it until dusk is falling."

They were surrounded by chattering children and wives pressing coins on them. Crispin refused all money. "Glad to do it: it was our pleasure, wasn't it, Joslin?"

"It was," Joslin answered, and in truth those hours had given him sweet and unalloyed pleasure.

"The sun's high in the sky. We've lost the morning," said Crispin. "But we'll make Hereford by evening."

Soon they were on the road leading south-west from Worcester. Crispin wore his short sword at his waist, Joslin his father's dagger. No road was safe, even on a bright summer's morning.

Joslin asked Crispin more about his brother and sisters. "What was Luke like?" he said.

"Luke hurt me more than anyone in my life," Crispin answered. "How can I answer, when he was my own brother?"

"Try," said Joslin.

"When I was a little boy I idolized him. Oh, I loved my sisters well enough, especially Christina. I felt somehow closer to her than the others. I admired Madge, but I was slightly frightened of her. She was tall and strong. She hunted with Luke. She had her own falcons and went hawking. She should have been born a boy. I wished she thought more of me. I can't understand how or why Luke managed to shut her away. But to me, Luke could do no wrong. He taught me to fight, hunt, look after myself. I owe him so much. And yet he wrecked my life, cast me adrift. Why, why, why?" He rode on, silent. Then he said, "But now's the time for reckoning."

They passed settlements and tiny villages, some deserted and ruined. They saw few people. The plague had hit hard here and numbers were still few.

The mountains to the west looked like the shoulders of giants dressed in mauve. The sun shone from a clear sky. When it was at its highest, they reached Bromyard. They drank ale and ate bread and cheese in a small tavern, then moved on.

In the late afternoon, Crispin said, "My brother's lands, which should be half mine, are over there." He pointed to his right.

Joslin saw great towers on the horizon. "Is that the cathedral?" he said. "Are we nearly in Hereford?"

"We are. You can see the cathedral, and behind it on its high hill, the castle."

The road turned to the left. They passed a clump of rowan trees.

"To the right is Luke's manor, to the left, St Katherine's nunnery," said Crispin.

"Are we stopping and going to your brother's manor?" Joslin asked.

"No," said Crispin. "It's a temptation. I could sort everything out in no more than a night. But it might also be the ruin of all I've waited for. I've learnt enough these last years to do things cautiously. We'll go into the city, keep our ears open and see how the land lies."

Joslin was glad. It was what he would have done. Besides, he knew enough about Crispin to be sure that, though he was daring, he never took unnecessary risks. As they neared the city they saw almost the first signs of life on the road since leaving Bromyard. One man pulled and two men pushed a small cart. A young priest walked in front, head bowed, hands together. Behind walked an older man, grave, dressed in a grey cloak. On the cart lay a shape under a shroud, unmistakably a body.

Joslin and Crispin were overtaking. But as they reached the cart they slowed, bowed their heads and made the sign of the cross. When they had passed, neither spoke. Crispin's face was impassive, but Joslin wondered how he regarded this welcome to his home city.

The cart with the dead man was left behind. Joslin and Crispin rode together down a widening street with tall timber frame houses each side, some empty. "This is Bye Street Without the Gates," said Crispin. "The city wall is ahead. Before the plague, the town was so wealthy it burst its bounds. When the plague went, one in three of its people were dead. When it came again, seven years ago, a year before I left, half the rest died. No Thurn was touched: it was the only merciful thing to happen to our family. Where there were once three thousand souls in Hereford, there were afterwards barely a thousand. You'll see the signs."

"There's one less now," Joslin replied and then wished he hadn't.

They came to a massive, square gate, built in brick, flanked either side by a high brick city wall. "Byster's Gate," Crispin said. Through the gate, the road forked, with Bye Street to their right and Grope Lane to the left. They rode on down Bye Street.

"St Peter's Street makes the other side of the

triangle," said Crispin. "Everything in between is Hightown, the market place."

Joslin saw more high, narrow buildings. Some were still shops. Others were in ruin. He noticed few people – nearly as many friars, both Greyfriars and Blackfriars, as ordinary folk. At the far end, facing St Peter's Street, was a church. "All Hallows," said Crispin.

"What shall we do?" asked Joslin.

"Walk, keep our eyes and ears open, and listen," Crispin replied.

So they did. They found an inn near the market place, made friends with the landlord, claimed lodging for the night, then went into the inn yard to see the horses stabled and fed.

"So let's look at Hereford, for what it's worth now," said Crispin. "I expect it's changed for the worse."

They left the inn and walked down High Street and Broad Street. Joslin's harp was on his back. He noticed that Crispin carried his flute. Minstrels were always ready to sing. They walked round the small city, then entered the precincts of St Ethelbert's cathedral. They saw the west tower and the huge central tower with scaffolding round it, the masons' lodge, tool store and hoists with hairy rope hauling up stones and buckets of mortar. Men in dusty smocks swarmed round the scaffolding and the top of the tower.

"So Hereford is not so plague poor that they can't work on their cathedral," said Crispin.

"Let's go inside," said Joslin.

They entered through the great west door and stood in the nave. Joslin was awestruck by its height, where the sweep of the complicated roof was lost in half darkness. Light filtered in subtle colours through the stained-glass windows. A steady shuffle of pilgrims passed through and disappeared into the north transept. "They're going to St Thomas Cantilupe's shrine," said Crispin. "He was once a bishop here and Hereford's very own saint, in the days when the city meant something."

A Mass was being said in a far chapel off the nave: Joslin heard the familiar words recited by a young voice. They stopped and waited quietly, while pilgrims and worshippers passed up and down the nave and negotiated the fencing placed round the foot of the long ladder in the crossing, close to a column in the corner. As Joslin watched, a workman climbed quickly up it, a bucket of mortar in one hand, and disappeared into the misty darkness of the roof.

Once again, Arthur was hurrying through a Mass. His mind was not on it. As he gave out the Host, he looked carefully at each person who came up to receive it. *No, not you. Not you. Nor you, neither. There's none of you I can talk to.* All these faces looked back at him blankly, saying silently "You're the priest. I come to you. You don't come to me."

The Mass finished. He watched the little flock disperse, then went to the sacristy and disrobed. His despair was complete. There was nobody here he could speak to and nobody in the rest of the world either. It was foolish even to think of that young traveller. What was he, but a face glimpsed for a moment, out of his life as soon as he was seen? In his anguish, an absolute conviction came to Arthur. That young man *would* have been the one, he *would*. But he was gone for ever. There would never be a soul to share his torment with.

But, when he was out in the nave, as pilgrims and worshippers swirled round him, he suddenly saw the one he sought. There was no mistake – the young traveller and his older companion were standing near the crossing, looking up at the great arch as if God had placed them there, ready to be met. Arthur spoke aloud to himself and pilgrims looked up in surprise. "Yes, *you*," he said. "I can talk to *you*."

But how could he meet them? He could hardly walk up to strangers and say, "I have a problem." No, he must make contact as any priest would to strangers, out of his duty both to God and to them.

Twenty or so people came out of the chapel when the Mass was over. A few minutes later Joslin saw a young priest following. The priest hesitated, then walked straight towards the minstrels. He had a pale, drawn face and dark-ringed, sunken, haunted eyes.

"I see you're strangers," the priest said. Before Crispin could say, "I'm not," the priest continued, "St Thomas Cantilupe's shrine is there, in the north transept," and pointed to the right of the crossing.

"We don't want St Thomas Cantilupe's shrine," Crispin growled. "I've seen it more times than you've got hairs on your chin."

That means not very often, Joslin thought. This priest couldn't be much older than he was and his beard looked even sparser. He remembered the students he knew best in the few days he was in Oxford: Roderick, Ralph, Arthur and Alfred. This priest would have fitted in well with them.

Crispin turned away. But the priest was persistent.

"I see you're both minstrels," he said.

"What of it?" said Crispin.

"I've not heard much music in this city since I've been here," the priest said. "I miss it. In Oxford, music seemed to be everywhere."

Joslin nearly said, "I never noticed, except when I played myself," but thought better of it. Instead he said, "Life can't be lived without it."

The priest looked at him in surprise. "You're from France," he said. "I can tell." His voice sounded wistful. "I've been there. I've seen Paris, Chartres, Orleans and Rheims. Fine cities with wonderful cathedrals." Then he said, as if it was a duty, "Almost as fine as this one."

"I know," said Joslin.

The priest awkwardly extended his right hand. "My name is Arthur," he said. "Arthur Rawle. I'm the bishop's chaplain. I count for nothing in this place."

Joslin felt the priest was saying anything to stop them leaving. He looked again at his pale face. Something was worrying him. If he wanted to tell somebody, then two minstrels, one French, would be strange choices. "I see," he said awkwardly.

"Have you got something to tell us?" said Crispin curtly.

A look almost of fear crossed the priest's face. "Tell you? No. What should I want to tell you?" he said. He turned away and walked quickly back towards the crossing and the choir.

"Why did you do that?" said Joslin. "The poor man was troubled. We should have let him speak on."

Crispin laughed explosively, so pilgrims stopped and looked at him. "Priests are supposed to be there for you to talk to *them*, not them to you," he said. "I'm getting out of here. This place depresses me. "

He turned on his heel and strode back out of the west door. Joslin waited a moment, hoping the young priest would come back. He had a feeling that the poor man wanted to ask for help, but didn't know how to. Now it was too late. The priest had disappeared, so Joslin followed Crispin outside.

Arthur was furious with himself. If only the older man hadn't frightened him off. But the Frenchman – yes, Arthur knew that he could be a friend, would understand, might even help. He must know the ways of the world, else why would he be in England in such troublous times? He went back into the chapel and knelt in front of the altar to pray. He stood up again at once. He had to see where they were going and prayers weren't likely to show him.

Edwin Pendock was in a room in the upper floor of Byster's Gate looking at the body of the man found wedged in the rowan trees. He shuddered. Yes, the poor fellow had fallen from a great height all right. How else could a human body be transformed into such a mere bag of bones? The limbs were so shattered that it was as if he'd been thrown down once, picked up, taken back and thrown down again. The face was smashed out of all recognition. He looked at the smock for marks which might show if the man had hit the ground on his back or his front. His eyes narrowed. There were marks of dust ingrained into the back and pieces of earth, grass and leaves still sticking to the cloth even after its time on the cart. On the front there was nothing, except for the unrecognizable face.

What did that mean? Perhaps something very sinister. He was sure the face was not made unrecognizable by hitting the ground first. It had been deliberately beaten. Why? To make sure nobody recognized it?

He peeled the smock off and examined the livid bruised skin. Once again, the worst marks were on the back. Yes, that was further proof. Whether before or after death, this face had been viciously hit and turned into a pulpy mess nobody would ever know. But Abel had said something about the set of the jaw being familiar. On the right upper arm was a jagged, livid scar. Edwin looked at it closely. It had nothing to do with his death. That scar was months old and well-healed.

He called downstairs for men of the watch. "I've seen all I can," he said. "Take him to the priest at St Peter's. Let the body lie there for two days. If nobody comes to claim him, he must be buried unknown."

Three men carried the body away. Edwin stayed, thinking. Who might know anything of this? The rowan trees were opposite Luke Thurn's lands. Edwin could not remember when he last saw Luke. They'd never been on the best of terms. There were rumours about how he had treated his young brother and that he had built a stone tower, to defend himself, it was said, against that brother's revenge which would surely come one day. He knew that one sister was married to a Welshman. For all he knew the other was as well. The fortunes of the Thurn family had never concerned him. Perhaps they should have.

Thurn must be visited. He had arranged with Hubert that next morning he would examine the ladder and the place where Christina was presumably thown off. He would go to Luke Thurn's before that. But Thurn's wasn't the only house on the city's north side. On the other side of the road, nearly a mile to the west, beside the road to Caerleon, was the House of the Blackfriars. He always felt awkward with friars, especially over matters like this, but they too would have to be seen.

Right, who first? He fished in his gown for a coin. "Heads, Luke Thurn: tails, the friars," he said. He flicked the coin in the air. Heads. Thurn. Well, get them all over with. Tomorrow.

Arthur pushed his way through the throng. Many muttered abuse until they saw he was a priest. If Giles or Ivo de Trellick could see him now he'd probably be packed out of Hereford at once and banished to the meanest parish they could find. But they didn't see him and he kept running until he was out of the cathedral and in the city streets.

The two would be here somewhere. If they were strangers, they'd most likely stay in a inn. Inns fit to lodge in were round the market place in Hightown. So he dashed up Mill Lane, down a narrow alley into St Peter's Street, across it and into Grope Lane. He saw no minstrels.

He ran back the other way, and looked up Bye Street.

Was that them he saw, just going into a large tavern? He was nearly sure. So he walked cautiously towards the doors and when he reached them, hesitated, because he was a priest at St Ethelbert's and the bishop's chaplain and this was not where he should be seen.

It didn't matter. He had to talk to this man. He burst

through the door and shouted, "Where are the minstrels? I have to see them."

At last. Arthur was face to face with this stranger in whom he had such confidence. He launched into what he wanted to say and gabbled without stopping. Even the older minstrel leaned forward and listened.

When he finished, he paused for breath. Joslin spoke. "Just a minute. Have I got this right? This morning you found a nun dead under the tower, as if she'd been thrown off it. In the afternoon, you found a dead man wedged in rowan trees, who looked as though he'd been thrown off a tower as well. Last night you had a nightmare you can't remember, but it's left you with a feeling that you're a murderer without knowing, so you feel guilty, but you don't know why."

"Yes," said Arthur.

"Who were these dead people?" said Crispin.

"Nobody knows the man. His face had been battered to pulp. Yet one of the masons says there's something about it which he knows. The nun was from St Katherine's. I seemed to recognize her."

"I knew that nunnery once," said Crispin.

"The nun's name was Christina."

Crispin sat bolt upright. "Are you sure?" he cried.

"Of course I am. Agatha the prioress said so."

"But that's my sister's name," cried Crispin. "It can't be her. She's not a nun." Then he slumped forward. "But she might have become a nun and I never knew. It would be like her to go." He pulled himself together and said, "Describe her to me."

"She was young. She might once have been pretty."

"That's right. She was – is," said Crispin."

"Though it was cut short, her hair was thick and lustrous."

"It is, it is. Everyone admires it," said Crispin.

"But though she was young, it was pure white."

"Oh, blessings on you, blessings from above for saying that." Crispin jumped up and hugged Arthur. "It's all right. My sister's hair was jet black. She's not your dead nun and I thank God for it."

Arthur walked slowly back to St Ethelbert's Cathedral. He had only been gone an hour. With luck, nobody had missed him.

Had the minstrels helped? When the elder was sure Christina was not his sister, he was sympathetic. He said, "I know what it is to be hemmed in by things you don't understand and can't do anything about." The younger asked a question which rocked Arthur back on his heels. "When you had your nightmares, did you walk in your sleep?"

"How did you know?" Arthur gasped.

"I didn't. But I've seen it before when I was a boy. Poor souls who walked at night all unknowing round the castle and sometimes fell to their deaths from the walls. Who knows what we do or what we see when we walk abroad without knowing?"

"If I walk in my sleep it means I did kill Christina." Arthur felt a choking despair.

"Not at all," said the young minstrel. "If you are a good man, then you won't do evil in your sleep."

"I try to be a good man," Arthur answered. "My parents told me that when I was small I walked while I slept. But a priest hauled that devil out of me and nothing like it has happened since."

"Perhaps that devil has returned," the young minstrel murmured.

"Pray God no," Arthur replied.

"Or perhaps it's no devil. Perhaps this is a way to find out what happened. Perhaps you might be able to unlock your mind's secrets, see through your sleep, and yourself become the scourge of evil."

"How can that be?" Arthur groaned.

The minstrel's reply was something Arthur would not forget. "When things happen that are beyond reckoning, and everyone and everything beats down as if the world wants an end of you, but you know you've done no wrong, be sure there's a way free to take if only you can find it." Arthur knew these weren't easy words to fob him off. The minstrel went on. "I've met people these last months who have done murder. I know in my heart that you're not one of them."

"That's enough for me," said Arthur. "You've given me much to think on. But I've been away from my duties too long. Thank you."

"We'll meet again," said the young minstrel. "Be sure of that."

As he closed the door he heard the elder say. "What do you mean, 'We'll meet again'? Don't make promises to strangers, Joslin. Remember our business here."

The younger replied. "I think he may be part of our business, Crispin. Two murders the moment we arrive? Don't tell me that's mere providence after all we've been through."

So those were their names – Joslin and Crispin. Odd that he hadn't thought to ask. But his mind was a little easier now.

St Katherine's nunnery was in ferment. Agatha was nowhere to be found. Sister Joan was distraught. She babbled her story to Freya, the manciple. "Agatha asked for Daw after we buried Christina. She wouldn't say where she was going. But it's to do with Christina." The old lady covered her face with her hands. "First Christina dead, now Agatha gone away," she wailed. "What is happening to us?"

"Have no fear," said Freya. "The Lord will return Agatha to us."

By evening, though, the Lord had only returned half the pair. As the sun sank, Daw trotted back alone, his harness trailing, and nobody knew what to do next.

After Arthur was gone and Crispin had warned him against making promises, Joslin was troubled. "Wherever I go, murder follows," he said. "Every town is riddled with it, as if it waits for me."

Crispin answered, "Not for much longer. When we've reached the ends of our journeys, we'll see no more of murder."

"If we ever reach them," Joslin replied.

"You've travelled in hope long enough," said Crispin. "Just as I have. Don't despair now."

"But *murder*. The worst thing that men can do," said Joslin. "When we find it, we have to clear it away."

"Only when it's our business. These murders are not our business. I've come to claim my rights and you're helping me. Nuns thrown off towers and serfs wedged in rowan trees have nothing to do with us."

"You're so sure of that," said Joslin. "I hope you can afford to be."

"I can afford anything I say I can," Crispin said.

"The priest asked for help," Joslin replied. "We must give it to him, as a good priest would give to us. I should go back to the cathedral to find out what he means."

"That you won't," Crispin replied. "It's none of our business."

"Are you so sure that the dead nun isn't your sister?" said Joslin.

Crispin did not answer. He sighed and said, "I know you well enough by now. If you get something in your head you'll worry at it like a dog with a rabbit. Have a good night's sleep and think again tomorrow. If you still want to, then go. But I'll not come with you."

"Why not?" said Joslin.

"Isn't it obvious? I'm here to meet Luke and meet Luke I will."

Edwin was not pleased to have a caller, as he at last sat down to dinner with family and household. But when told it was Sister Freya, the manciple from St

Katherine's, and old Sister Joan with her, he stood up at once. He knew Freya as a calm woman well able for any day-to-day crisis and Joan to be ancient, if not wise. He was not prepared for the distraught women he saw.

"We're sorry to disturb you," said Freya. "It's God's business we come on. Joan has things to tell."

Joan stammered out her news. "Sister Agatha's little pony came trotting back and into his stable with the secret of where he left her in his eyes, but no way of telling us."

"I hope you don't think I can talk to horses," Edwin replied.

Joan's face seemed to say that, after so many years in the nunnery, nothing those in the world outside could do would surprise her. What's more, she was rather hoping he could.

"I assure you that I can't," he said quickly.

"What will you do?" Freya pleaded.

"I must think. There's no point in running into the dark looking for her. I must know what I seek. I'll be at the nunnery tomorrow. I'll tell you then."

"Must that content us?" said Freya. "With all the cares of St Katherine's on my shoulders, must I have so little comfort for my sisters?"

"For tonight. I can do no more now," Edwin replied. He spoke to a servant. "Show the sisters out with all respect and gentleness."

When they were gone, he sat in silence. Why should Agatha ride off on her own without telling anybody? There could be only one reason. She was unhappy with how he was treating Christina's murder and thought she could do better herself.

What would that mean? Either she was stupid,

which he knew she wasn't, or she had good reason to think she could. Perhaps she was right. Perhaps finding the second body so soon had sent him off on the wrong course. Instead of trying to find out more about Christina, he was carried away by wondering about why the dead man should be left stuck in the rowan trees.

The more he thought about it, the more he cursed himself. He was wrong. He should have concentrated on Christina. She was the victim for whom they had a name and a place to start at. He should have spent more time talking to Agatha. Agatha might not know everything about her, but she might know enough to suggest reasons why the poor girl should suffer such a terrible death.

But now Agatha had gone as well and he was left to berate himself for being a bumbling fool. What a day tomorrow would be! Thurn, Blackfriars, Hubert, now St Katherine's. But Thurn was first. He had a nagging feeling that something important was to be found there.

What was that feeling? Why not try to put flesh on it?

Right. The body in the rowans was dumped opposite Thurn's place. Why? Murder was surely a secret thing, yet this body was left for all to see – or such few as might be on the road from Worcester.

Who had seen it? Arthur and the masons. They couldn't miss it with that dangling arm. When he came back with them, the body was still there. But this time it had been stuffed out of sight. If they hadn't seen it before, they wouldn't have known.

Arthur and the masons said two horsemen passed by as they found the body, made disparaging remarks about Hereford welcomes and rode on. So they must have had nothing to do with it. But what about those other two travellers who overtook them near Byster's Gate? Were *they* meant to find the body? No, not with the arm tucked away.

But what if he hadn't gone to bring the body to Hereford? What if someone pulled the arm out again and the travellers saw it? Would they know the man despite his ruined face? What would they do? Raise the alarm in Hereford? Tell them at St Katherine's? Tell Luke Thurn?

A body left for some to see. Just as Christina's was. Two dead bodies in a few hours. Why, why, why?

Just think if the two travellers had seen it first, then turned in to St Katherine's and told them there. What would Agatha have said?

Then he groaned aloud. *Agatha wasn't there.* Would they find her body left in a public place as well?

Might the travellers have told Luke Thurn?

Then Edwin's hair at the back of his neck rose, and his heart beat faster. *What if Luke Thurn had put it there?* Which made another question rise up. *Who were the two travellers?*

Now he knew what he had to ask, so he felt able to sleep. He would be up at the crack of dawn. He had to get this over with.

For a long time Joslin lay sleepless on his straw mattress and pallet. So many questions. . .

That talk with the young priest worried him deeply. He knew that what Crispin said about dogs, rabbits and his own thoughts was so true. But he couldn't help it. If he hadn't worried at problems till answers came he'd have been dead long since. So what had he learnt?

Arthur Rawle had a lot to worry about. A priest being a murderer without knowing? Very unlikely. Yes, but not impossible. Might he walk in his sleep and might that be a way for Satan to get inside him and make him do his will? Who knows what we do when we roam a world ruled by the spirit of dreams? What a bitter joke it would be if Satan used a priest? Nobody should laugh Arthur's fears away.

What did Arthur tell them about Christina? A young nun with white hair. Crispin seemed certain she was not his Christina. But how old was she when he last saw her? Fourteen? Fifteen? That would make her twenty-four now. Very young to have white hair, especially when Crispin described the hair he remembered as "jet black".

The hair was the reason Crispin said this nun couldn't be his sister. But something must have happened to send her to a nunnery? The last Crispin knew, she was waiting for Luke to find her a fit husband.

White hair, white hair. Those words ran through his mind like a strange chorus to a weird song. What would make jet black, lustrous – that was what Arthur had called it – hair turn white before the age of twenty-four? Hard work? Well, as a novice she'd get plenty of that. Or something else, like a terrible shock? He'd heard tell of such things. But if so, it must have been a shock to pull the soul screaming from out of her body.

"Crispin," he said, not so loud that Crispin would wake up, "you're wrong. I'm afraid for you. That nun was your sister and she's dead. Before we go in a rush to get what you want from Luke you need to think hard. We have to talk to that priest. He doesn't know it, but I reckon his sleepwalking may be the key."

Crispin snored in answer.

Arthur was in his room in the bishop's palace. He looked out at the night scene – to his left, the cathedral's dark shape: to his right, the high black mound with the castle's silhouette on its top. Before, seeing that sight by moonlight had given him such pleasure; it meant church and king, the two pillars of the wonderful life in front of him.

Tonight, all was changed. The castle was a feature-less heap. The cathedral was not God's wonderful temple, but a place of terror. No matter how the young minstrel tried to calm him, Arthur had this devil's feeling stuck inside him that the poor nun's death was *his* fault and so, by some calculation he couldn't understand, but knew must be true, was the murder of the man in the rowans. He was nothing now but a lost, lost soul.

That night, he ate with the bishop as always. But he had no appetite. Giles saw and spoke kindly. "Arthur," he said. "I know that what happened in our lovely church is a terrible thing. But God will make it right and you must be patient for that to happen. So eat and be yourself, the strong fine priest I brought here as my chaplain."

"My lord," Arthur muttered. But it wasn't easy when you *knew*.

Now he was on his own, in the dark, locked in with thoughts rising like precipices too steep to climb and too high to look down without shivering dread of falling. He knelt at the foot of his bed, but knew his prayers went nowhere. What hour was it? He had no idea. Owls hooted outside and bats flitted past like the damned from hell come to taunt him, like his inmost fears made flesh. The night would be very long.

Yet somehow he drifted into sleep, slumped awkwardly across the end of his bed.

Edwin found it difficult to sleep and the easy breathing of his comfortable wife only made it harder. He tried to find connections between the strange events – Christina's death, the strange man's death, the terrible thing done to his face, Agatha's disappearance. Nothing worked. But if such things happened with one so quick on top of the next, yet with nothing to do with each other, then Providence's wheel was so buckled there was no point any more to his job of seeking truth through the connections in events.

What would he find at Luke Thurn's place tomorrow morning? Those odd rumours about trouble there over the years – as Justice of the Peace, why hadn't he investigated them properly? He should have. It was no use saying that Thurn lived three miles out of Hereford and nobody bothered about such a distance. Thurn was a Hereford man and so was his father. Old Simon had often worshipped at St Ethelbert's as well as St Peter's, his nearest city church. He remembered a quarrel between the brothers. Then there was the marriage between the eldest daughter and that Welshman. In the chapel of the Blackfriars, wasn't it? How many years ago was that? And afterwards, there was all the building Luke wanted done when he extended the house. He turned a perfectly good dwelling into some sort of castle. Was it really to defend himself against his brother? Or was it just the folly of a rich man? Well, riches make some men do strange things. There were a lot of rumours about Thurn's new building – and a lot of anger in Hereford as well. Very few local masons had worked there, at a time when there wasn't much work in the city, and none of them had come home afterwards. And now – was Thurn at home like a hermit, as some said, or was he still on that long journey, like his younger brother who had been away for years? Rumours, rumours, rumours. Why hadn't he got to the bottom of them? Edwin sighed. The Thurns were his concern and not knowing their business meant he had fallen down in his duty.

The questions whirled round inside his head and

For Crispin, in these lonely hours when night thoughts are at their worst, awful suspicions about Christina's fate coursed through his brain. "You didn't believe them last night and when day comes you still won't believe them," he told himself. The ugly demon in his skull answered, "Then why are you believing them now, Crispin?"

"Be quiet," he said aloud and tried to sleep again. More hours passed before he managed it.

Arthur had sat stunned and unbelieving in the cathedral nave for a long time. His limbs and joints seemed frozen. The first streaks of dawn showed before he began to thaw like a block of ice, rise and walk stiffly, like an old man, out of the west door and into chill air.

Edwin slept well now his mind was made up. Ulf, on his mattress of rags in the masons' lodge, slept fitfully, because he had not got over Hubert and Edwin being suspicious of him about the ladder. It wasn't *really* his fault that the killer took it.

Ulf woke suddenly. Was someone coming? He

listened. Yes, there were footsteps outside. He jumped up and peered outside, making sure nobody could see him. Someone in a nightgown was stumbling past. This person looked like – who? Ulf could only think of his old grandfather, who died full of years and almost bent double.

The thought of his grandfather coming back was strangely comforting. He lay down again and slept. But then he had bad dreams about when his mother died in the plague and his father was found murdered in Grope Lane, and when he woke up with the first light his face was wet with tears.

When Arthur woke that morning, his first sound was a whimper. His worst imaginings were true. He *did* walk in his sleep, even if he had stumbled consciously back to the bishop's palace and his bedchamber. This meant he *had* thrown that poor, innocent nun to her death without knowing what he was doing. So the devil himself was curled up inside him, had made a poor young priest's frail body his home. This devil slept by day, but woke at night and *became* him. What could he do?

Even as he asked, he knew there was no answer. This wasn't a sin to confess to his bishop and receive forgiveness. *It was what he was.*

Besides, what would happen if he did confess? Giles Longland would recoil as if from a monster spitting poison, such as those the travellers who had walked the far lands shown on the Mappa Mundi told of. He would cry, "Get thee behind me, Satan." Then what? Arthur could not imagine.

He couldn't tell anybody. Except Joslin. Well, at least he knew which tavern he was staying in. But

Joslin had business of his own, without bothering about the travails of an obscure English priest. Oh, it was all hopeless. His life was as good as over.

But the morning's early Mass called him. Even if he was just a shell of what he should be, his duties had to be done. So he pulled his clothes on and shambled off towards the cathedral. He was deathly pale. There were dark rings round his sunken eyes. Perhaps Giles would take one look and banish him from St Ethelbert's for ever.

Actually, at that moment he rather hoped he would.

Joslin woke. "What's next to do today?" he asked.

"I'm not wasting my time with dead nuns and sad priests," Crispin answered. "We're off to my brother's place to see how the land lies." He laughed, then continued. "*My* place is what I should have said."

"I hope you're right," said Joslin. "But I have my doubts."

Crispin's face darkened. "Why should you have doubts?" he roared. "It's not your concern to have doubts about my business."

Joslin would not be cowed by his anger. "You heard what Arthur said last night. I hope with all my heart that the dead nun isn't your sister. But I have bad thoughts about it."

Crispin's anger died. "I'm not sure," he answered. "I've thought about it all night, and the more I think, the more I fear. There's only one way to clear it up. See Luke. Find out what's happened while I've been away. Settle our differences now."

"What will you say to him? What if he sets his dogs on us? Or his men? That would be worse. Remember what Gamelyn's brother did to him in the ballad. I don't want to be a prisoner in Luke's house and neither do you. It would be mad if your quest ended the moment you set foot in the place."

Crispin was silent. Then he said, "You're right, Joslin. You always are and I get tired of it sometimes. But I'll take notice. We'll go to my brother's place this morning because we have to. But we'll be careful."

Joslin didn't answer. He was thinking about what lay before him – entry into a strange house from which they might not come out alive. He remembered other times he had done this. Then he shuddered. Something about the prospect brought back when he and Alys had got into the castle at Stovenham, through the old tunnel made years before by King John's soldiers. And that awful fear he had then came flooding back – no air, unable to breathe, pitch darkness, the thought of such weight of earth and stone pressing the life out of him Why should he remember this now?

He told Crispin, expecting to be mocked. But Crispin did no such thing. "I can well imagine what you mean," he said. "It's like something I've feared all my life. It's a fear I shared with Christina. Another reason why Luke had no time for me."

"Tell me about it," said Joslin. "I've told you my fears."

Crispin screwed up his eyes as if he was in pain. Then he said, "When Christina was a little girl she woke up screaming one night. She told us she had a dream of being walled up alive. She saw the stones rise in front of her, heard the tapping of trowels as they were put in place and then, just as the last was mortared in, she woke up. I remember Luke was angry, and said he would take her to a priest. Madge laughed and thought it was funny. I thought about it

– and then thought and thought and thought until I couldn't get it out of my head. Since then, no matter what danger I face and laugh at, that's the one thing I have real bad dreams about. Airless tunnels, closed-up walls. What's the difference? You and I share a horror, Joslin."

Hubert was glad to see nobody had interfered last night with the tool store. With any luck, today's work would pass uninterrupted.

He made the masons go to early Mass with him. Arthur looked half-dead and his voice saying Mass was inaudible. Giles Longland and Ivo de Trellick had faces like thunder. Before they reached the psalm for the day, Ivo left his stall, pulled Arthur away, pushed the nearest canon in his place and hissed, "You get on with it and make a better job than he did." The canon started saying the Mass but stammered over his words as if he feared Ivo's fury was aimed at him. But Hubert saw well that it wasn't. Arthur slumped forward as if in a dead faint. Hubert wanted to help him, but under the glare of both bishop and dean did not dare move. The masons behind him muttered. He heard Abel whisper, "Poor lad, He's seen enough to turn his mind these last days."

The first cocks were crowing when Edwin rose. He left his wife asleep and stumbled blearily downstairs. He stood in the courtyard outside the stables and shouted, "Wake up." No one came. He marched into the dark stables and shouted again. "Where are you?"

Two stable lads appeared, hardly awake. "Saddle my second best horse, the grey," he commanded. "Then bring it out to me."

Ten minutes later he was on his way up Broad Street, into Bye Street and through Byster's Gate. On horseback, the going was much faster than yesterday with the masons' cart. Three miles out and opposite the sinister rowan trees he came to Luke Thurn's manor house.

As he rode, he put together again all he knew about Luke Thurn. The family had little to do with Hereford since the younger son went away. There was some trouble then and rumours about the old man's death had spread, then died as such things will with no fuel to keep them alive. He seemed to remember something about trouble later on, but what it was he had no idea. If Thurn had come back from the journey he was rumoured to be on and really was living the life of a hermit, then he must be in that house, lording it over serfs on their strips of land for all the world like a small baron.

He turned his horse off the road and they walked up the track past high, unkempt trees. Thurn's lands were going to rack and ruin. Everything near was overgrown and untended, but trim plots not far away showed how his tenants could look after their own interests. Yet they were deserted. Surely by now men should be at work.

He approached the house itself. It was large, solid, timber-framed like those in the city, with a great hall, solar and undercroft for storage. Luke either had ambitions to be a local magnate able to strike fear into folk, or he was a frightened man. For circling the house was a ditch, a miniature moat such as a castle has. Beyond was a fence made of strong wooden palisades. It reminded Edwin of the walls the Normans built round a motte and bailey before they built stone walls in their place. He had seen the remains of some. Facing him was a drawbridge, drawn up. At the end of the hall away from the solar, was the tower itself, which had so angered un-employed Hereford masons. Edwin had often seen it from the road: now he was close, he looked at it care-fully. Its grey stone contrasted with the wattle and daub of the timber-framed house. It was square, with a battlemented and turreted top and arrow slits round the sides, for all the world like a tiny castle keep.

Then a new thought came. A *tower*. Was this the first glimmer in the fog? A man is found dead, probably thrown from a great height, and left by the road close by. And here was a tower to throw him from.

Edwin looked at tower, moat and drawbridge and wondered what ambitions or fears made Luke build them. The house was fairly new. Edwin was young when the plague came to Hereford for the first time. He had survived it, as he had the second. But he remembered others who had survived, yet lost everything, like ruined, lonely Sir Redvers Maylord who gave half his land and manorial rights away to his bailiff, old Simon Thurn, who then built himself that fine house. But when Simon had finished it, that was all it was – just a house.

Could there be a reason for moat, drawbridge and tower that he didn't know of? Since the treaty between the English and Welsh a hundred years before, Hereford had been quiet, no more a war town which was the last line of defence and first stage of attack. No one threatened the city. Was Luke getting ready to fight a private war? Possibly. Such things happened, for all the efforts of justices to stop them. But who against? His brother? Was his brother likely to return with an army? Besides, what use were castle keeps without garrisons in them? This one was as silent as the tombs in St Ethelbert's. Was Thurn inside?

He had to get right up to the house. Though the drawbridge was up, the moat was dry and the few reeds were parched. He could pick his way across. It was not wide compared with the moat round Hereford Castle in the days when it was ready for war.

He tied his horse to a nearby sapling and lowered himself into the ditch. The banks were as high as a small man. The moat's floor squelched slightly. He struggled six paces to the far edge, pulled himself up and found a ledge under the fence big enough to stand on. Then he swung himself up and dropped down the other side. Edwin then spoke aloud to himself, as he often did when a problem showed itself. "The army Luke's expecting must be very small."

He looked round. He stood in an overgrown mess. Weeds and creepers straggled everywhere. From this side, the defensive wall looked more like a hedge, so dense was it with tangled creepers. He pushed his way to the house, then round it. There was still no sign of life. He looked in the undercroft. Rusty ploughs, harrows and billhooks were scattered around the floor as if the land was abandoned for ever. He looked for a door. There was the great door to the house itself, which he remembered from old Simon's days, and one to the tower, from which a stone path led to the drawbridge. Both doors were sturdy and fast bolted. He hammered on them, first the tower, then the house. He called. "Luke Thurn. Come out and show yourself." No answer.

He turned away. The house was empty. Yet suddenly, some instinct came, some pricking of the thumbs, which told him it was not.

He hammered on the tower door and shouted again. "Thurn. Luke Thurn. Are you there? Come on out." Again, no answer.

He walked round the house again. Then he explored the courtyard at the back. He peered in empty stables, echoing barns. Nothing.

In the middle of the courtyard was a well. It had a wooden roof on the very point of collapse. The rope on the windlass was broken: a frayed end hung uselessly. There was no bucket. Edwin peered over the well's edge. The stone-lined well shaft was deep and very dark. He thought he could see, far, far below, a sullen glint of water as if some slimy blind beast moved underneath it. For some reason he could not explain, he called to it. "Hallo down there!" His voice returned, a strange, small echo. He shuddered at the thought of overbalancing, scrabbling hopelessly, then falling into water shared by that creature.

Quickly he straightened up, turned away and breathed the blessed dry air deeply. He took one more turn round the courtyard. The only movement came from scurrying rats and nesting owls angry at being woken. Then he looked back at the house. There was no sign of human life. Just plain desertion. Or so it appeared. And yet he knew somebody was there, somewhere. Was it Luke? If it was, why wouldn't he come out? What did he have to hide?

Obviously he wouldn't find out this morning. It seemed he had to cross Luke Thurn off his list of suspects – for now, at least. He returned to the tower door and then followed the path to the drawbridge.

He looked at it. It was lifted by a rope which, unlike the well's rope, was new and intact. He found the handle of the windlass and tried to turn it. Strange. This drawbridge had been looked after. And it was up when he found it. So Luke was inside and he wanted no visitors.

He turned the handle a few times. The only creaking came from the dry rope. He stopped and started turning it back.

Then he spoke aloud again. "No. Why should I? Whoever's in there might not want to see me, but he's not going to stop me going." So he lowered the drawbridge, stepped across, untied his horse and rode away, thinking deeply.

It would be a warm day. Sweat trickled down the back of Edwin's neck as he entered Hereford and made his way to his house in Bridge Street. He was in a bad temper. After the strange but fruitless visit to Thurn's small castle his horse had picked its way along a narrow track which led to the Caerleon Road while he had sat on its back musing. Then he had visited the Blackfriars.

They knew nothing. Except for one piece of information which might be useful. "Old Simon Thurn, always a good friend to us though I can't say the same about his elder son, is buried here, in our graveyard," the Abbot told him. "Luke asked for it and for Simon's sake we saw no reason to deny his wish. It was a long time ago now."

Did that tell him anything useful? Edwin didn't know. He reached his house, stabled his second best horse and set off for the cathedral and his appointment with Hubert.

As he passed the mason's lodge he saw Ulf's thin face watching him suspiciously, as if he thought

Edwin might steal the ladder himself. Well, suspicion like that was commendable if Ulf was to do his job well. It was just a pity that he hadn't shown it the night before last.

He came into the echoing nave of St Ethelbert's. Under the crossing he found Arthur Rawle waiting as well as Hubert. After Arthur's humiliation at early Mass, Ivo de Trellick had insisted on Arthur being there, perhaps as a punishment. "The Church must keep watch on the civil powers on holy ground," he said. "You're the very man to do it, Arthur. Perhaps it will help you." He must have seen mutiny in Arthur's face, as he added, "The bishop also commands it."

Well, Arthur *was* feeling mutinous. What happened last night still beat through his mind. He felt less terrified now than after he left the cathedral in the night, except that – and this made him shiver with new horror – if he was made to climb up this frail thread of a ladder, *he might realize that he had climbed it before. That could only mean one thing.* And then what would he do? Break down and confess to this crime, throw himself on a mercy which he would not be given?

However, there was nothing for it. He had to climb. Hubert had started, Edwin was waiting. He was to go in the middle. He put his foot tentatively on the first rung and with some effort coaxed the other on to the next. The climb was worse than he could imagine. He was toiling through empty air. Long before he reached the top he was fighting to keep his eyes open. He wanted to shut out both the dizzying drop below and the impossibly high roof above. The intricate chevroned tops of the round arches hurt his eyes to look at. They were meant to be seen from below, and that was where Arthur wished he was.

They reached solid stone and he breathed again. Then he saw another ladder ahead and he nearly gave up. But his bishop had commanded him so he kept going. He gasped, "Why didn't we go up the ladders on the scaffolding outside? They're much safer."

"Because I believe," said Edwin, "that poor Christina was lured up the ladder inside."

"That's right," said Hubert. "We said this yesterday morning. The ladder wasn't where we left it the night before and there's an end of it."

"That means nothing," said Arthur. He thought of Ulf and had a sudden impulse to keep him out of trouble – as well as himself. "Christina could still have gone up the scaffolding outside."

"I know I'm right," Edwin replied.

"How can you be sure?" said Arthur.

"I can't. It's just my feeling."

"I say Edwin speaks true," said Hubert. "You'd need a light to climb the scaffolding. That would risk being seen. If you didn't have a light, you'd risk kicking stones or tools and buckets left up there overnight. If you weren't seen, then you'd be heard. A lump of dressed stone or half a bucket of mortar hitting the ground could wake a lot of people up. Besides, you could fall down with them."

Leaving aside the fact that someone *had* fallen down, Arthur thought that even if that was true, it didn't seem enough to put him through this ordeal. He said so.

"This is my investigation, not the bishop's," said Edwin stiffly. "If I believe Christina was lured up here, I want to know exactly what happened. I want to see it with my own eyes."

So Arthur gritted his teeth, put horrors behind him and endured two more ladders, each mercifully shorter than the last. Now they felt a fresh wind through unfilled spaces in the walls. Arthur saw leering, half-comic faces of gargoyles fixed in the wall to gaze sardonically over Hereford for many centuries to come. As always when he saw such things, the priest in him made him frown. Should the church approve of such irreverent little demons?

Hubert saw his expression. "I hope you're not going to tell us to take them down," he said. "There's many hours from good craftsmen gone into them. And we aren't going to put any golden angels in their place, either."

"Golden angels?" said Arthur, puzzled. "What do you mean? Why should you put golden angels here?" Then he felt strange alarm: somehow angels had seemed to be part of his nightmare.

"Haven't you heard?" said Edwin. "I've never known a place like Hereford for rumours. There's one been going round that an angel, exquisitely carved and shining in pure gold, is to be put up here, to raise a trumpet over the city and be one of the great wonders of the world."

"That's news to me," said Arthur. "But I'm still new here. It would be wonderful if it was true." *Please God, let it not be*, he thought.

"There, you see, you're as bad as the rest of them," said Hubert. "No, it is not true. And I'd like to find out who spread that rumour, because it's caused me more trouble denying it over these last weeks than anything to do with the real building that's going on. I'm not having any angel, gold or otherwise, on my tower."

"Come on," said Edwin impatiently. "We must get to the top. I've a lot to do today."

They climbed the last ladder and stood at the tower's summit, where crenellated battlements were still being built and the pinnacles at each corner were half complete. Up here, the wind blew stronger and the sight of Hereford far below was dizzying. Arthur had to grab at a battlement.

"She must have gone on to the scaffolding and fallen from there," said Hubert. "Unless someone made her, why should she do that?"

"But there's a gap between the stone of the tower and the floor of the scaffolding," said Edwin. "Could she have fallen through it?"

"Never," said Hubert. "She'd have landed on the roof of the nave or the transepts. That could kill her, but her body would most likely have stayed on the roof. No, she fell from off the scaffolding."

"So did she slip, did she jump off deliberately or was she pushed?" said Arthur. If only it was the first or the second.

"She couldn't have come up here on her own," said Hubert. "She wouldn't know how. Someone guided her. Whoever it was threw her off at the top and meant her to land on the ground for all to see."

"It surely was a strong lure to make a nun break her bounds, walk three miles alone in the dark and climb these ladders," said Arthur. "What can it have been?"

"That's what I shall find out," said Edwin Pendock. "Someone in Hereford finds pleasure in throwing poor souls down great drops to their deaths, and we must find out who it is before more of us go the same way."

Well, his next calling place would have to be

St Katherine's. Even as he prepared to take his leave and go back to Bridge Street for his horse, he realized with a cold qualm that, unless Agatha came back soon, before very long there might be a third body.

As Edwin rode out to St Katherine's, something his father once told him rang in his ears. "There's more to these nuns than meets the eye." For years Edwin wondered what he meant. He knew nuns, friars and monks well enough – who could live in a cathedral city surrounded by friaries, monasteries and nunneries without knowing them – but he'd never had cause to deal with them when crimes were committed. What crimes could happen at St Katherine's? Today was a new experience and, for all his years in this job, Edwin felt apprehensive as he drew near the low stone buildings.

After two hours he had learnt even less than he feared. Joan was the only person who was sure when Agatha left and all she said was, "It was after we buried Christina. Agatha never said where she was going and I wouldn't ask." When Edwin said that surprised him, she answered, "She was my superior." When Edwin remarked that surely it was her duty to know where her prioress went, she answered with surprising spirit, "I am not my sister's keeper." The day's first sign that his father might have been right.

Edwin asked Freya to call everyone to the refectory at once. He had to speak to them. "Agatha would not like that," the manciple said.

"She's not here to object," Edwin replied. His patience was wearing thin. "If you want her safely back, then you really should listen to me."

When the nuns were gathered out of chapel, stable, cell, kitchen and garden, he looked at the extraordinary assortment in front of him. Fat, thin, young, old – sometimes very old. Some plain, some with beauty which caught at his heart and made him wonder what fortunes had brought them here. An aura of goodness rose from them – or was it his imagination? When he started his questions, he stumbled over his words as if he was a small boy with no right to speak in their presence.

No nun had any idea that Agatha had left St Katherine's until she was missed in the afternoon. "Are they really that unobservant or does a life of prayer make them blind to everything else?" Edwin wondered. There was nothing here to explain his father's opinion of nuns.

He tried again. "Has *nobody* any idea where your prioress might have gone?" Blank looks and head shakings all round. "*Why* might she have gone? Was she trying to find who killed Christina?" For the first time their faces showed they at least knew what he was talking about.

"Do you think the prioress might have an idea who did this terrible thing?" Edwin asked.

There was whispering all round the refectory and eyes looked at him as if he had said something awful. "What did I say that you mislike so much?" he cried.

The whispering stopped. A young nun near the front stepped forward. "Sir," she said. "Everyone here has a story to tell of why she came here. Some came out of a simple wish to be close to Christ and His mother. Some came because they were disappointed in marriage and knew they would have no more chances. Others came because they needed to escape from the world after some terrible mischance. But you must realize that none of us knows each other's story. We keep them to ourselves and take them to our graves. Even if we think we know the reasons which brought others here, we never ask and we never talk about them one to another as women in the world might. When we enter here, our lives start again. So there's no use your asking about things forgotten, even if they have risen again to strike at one of us."

Edwin looked at her with surprised respect. Yes, there was more to these nuns than met the eye. She had as good as said, "There's no point in your being here." He felt soiled, clumsy and an intruder.

"I see," he said. He looked at them in silence for a few moments. Then he said. "I'm sorry. You may leave."

They stood up, quiet and grave. As they filed out, they all inclined their heads towards him, a gentle dismissal.

But Freya stayed. "What my sister said was right, of course," she said. "Even so, I believe Agatha has a notion of why each of us comes. She never asks, but before they know our rule, new arrivals may say more than they mean. Agatha keeps such things close, but she may know where to start to find out Christina's story and to that place she might have gone."

"Why didn't she wait and tell me?" Edwin couldn't keep the irritation out of his voice.

"That she would never do," the manciple replied. "She would say confidences made to her are beyond the reach of the King's law you bring here. You would never ask a priest to say what he learns in confession. In the same way you must not ask her." Then she left, as quiet and grave as the others.

Edwin stood quivering with frustration. He was getting nowhere.

Then he realized that the refectory was not empty. Two nuns, both older than Christina was, with weatherbeaten faces and rough callused hands as if they had worked hard for many years, stood watching him. When he saw them, they approached him.

"Sir," said one. "We can't let you leave without telling you something."

"It's a curious event which we can't forget," said the other. "We've talked about it and decided you should know."

"Go on," said Edwin, not expecting to hear anything useful.

"We work together in the gardens," said one. "We grow all the food we eat."

"Yes, yes," said Edwin impatiently.

"I am Sister Mildred," said the first nun. "This is Sister Rosette."

"Lately, Christina worked with us," said Rosette. "We were teaching her all she would have to do in the garden, for we won't be here for ever."

"And yet it is Christina who has gone first," said Mildred.

"Tell me what you have to," said Edwin.

"There's an outhouse built of stone where we keep what we need for the garden," said Rosette. "About a month ago, we saw that one of the walls was crumbling. We told Freya. She said she would see to it."

"What's this got to do with it?" asked Edwin.

Mildred looked at him reprovingly. "You are a very hasty man," she said. "Haste is a sin of the world which has no place here."

Edwin sat on a bench feeling like a small, naughty boy. "I'm sorry," he said. "Please go on. I won't interrupt again."

"This was not a job any of us could do," said Rosette. "Freya brought a man in to repair the wall. He came with mortar and trowel and did a very good job. You can see it if you look."

"But he was a great one for talking," said Mildred. "We tried to close our ears to him, but it was no use. Christina was quite taken up by what he was saying – too much for our liking."

"He kept telling her about a golden angel," said Rosette. "I remember what he said even though I tried not to listen. 'Ah, that golden angel,' he said. 'It will live for ever at the wonderful place where Hereford reaches up and touches heaven itself, to keep watch over the city and everywhere around. I know it will. I've seen it for myself.' We tried to drag Christina away from him, but we couldn't. What he said had transfigured her, brought a look of such joy to her face."

" 'The golden angel,' she cried," said Mildred. " 'Oh, my wonderful golden angel. How I long to see it again.' The man answered, 'You shall. I know where it is and how to reach it.' After that, he finished his job, Freya paid him and he went. We never saw him again. But we knew Christina wouldn't rest until she'd seen this supposed golden angel and we feared for her."

"Did you tell your prioress?" Edwin asked.

The two looked guilty. Edwin wondered whether to try a reproving look as a little revenge but decided it was not right. "No," said Mildred. "We wouldn't speak ill of a nun to anyone, not even Agatha."

"Even though her soul might have been in danger," said Rosette.

"And her life," said Mildred. "But how could we know that?"

"We only told her we should take no notice of such vanities and that when they were told to us by such a one as him they could not come from God," said Rosette.

"What did she say to that?" Edwin asked.

"She said how could we know that anyone who brought news of a golden angel wasn't an angel himself in human shape," said Mildred.

"We couldn't think of an answer to that," said Rosette. "I've not slept for many nights worrying about it."

"Don't worry," said Edwin. "Ask your priest for forgiveness. He'll give it because I don't believe you've done wrong and neither will he. And I tell you that even though I'm just a rough man myself."

Relief flooded their faces. "Thank you," said Mildred. "We'll remember you in our prayers." They left, leaving him wondering whether this was a chink of light in the sorry business. He only had to find that man who said he could take Christina to the golden angel. . .

Before he left, he knocked on the door of the manciple's room. Freya was inside, poring over the accounts. "Who was the man who repaired the outhouse wall?" he asked.

Freya turned back through the accounts, her index

finger following her writing as she mouthed words and numbers to herself. "Here it is," she said finally. "'Four pence to Jude Cox, journeyman mason, for making good the side wall of the outbuilding by the kitchen garden. Paid on the eighth day of May.' Is that what you want?"

As he rode home, he pondered. "The wonderful place where Hereford reaches up to heaven." What did that mean?

Wasn't it obvious? The central tower of St Ethelbert's cathedral.

A journeyman mason, spreading that rumour about a golden angel. And not just telling it. What did Jude Cox say? "I've seen it for myself." Jude Cox must be more than a rumour-monger. But why say something so obviously untrue to someone who would have no hope of ever seeing it – and then spread a rumour about it around the city? No wonder Hubert Fennel told everyone that stories about a golden angel were a pack of lies. He couldn't risk a line of people climbing the tower while he was working there.

Yet Christina tried to climb it the night she died. So it wasn't true that she had no hope of seeing it. She was so fired by what this mason told her that she'd tried to – and all that stopped her, besides the fact that it wasn't there to start with, was whoever dashed her down to the hard ground dizzyingly far below. Who could know what she *had* seen up there, what blinding revelation of evil?

There was something here which he couldn't quite get hold of. He was so close to a clinching fact: he knew that what Mildred and Rosette had told him was important. *Jude Cox.* What a hard, stark name. He knew that nobody was called Jude after Judas Iscariot but the mere sound made him think of slippery guile, betrayal and treachery. And Jude Cox had betrayed Christina. Why should he pick her out to give his message to? Why was it so important that she broke her bounds and came to her death because of it? Most important of all, was Jude working alone or was he a messenger for someone even more sinister?

He was still thoughtful as he spurred his second best horse into a canter. But as he passed through Byster's Gate, he knew what to do first before he could find answers to these questions. He would see Hubert. Every man from miles around who called himself a mason had worked at the cathedral: if Jude Cox was a mason, Hubert would have employed him. Why, he might even still be there.

And if Hubert knew him, then Edwin knew exactly what to do next. He might even be near to solving the first part of this mystery and with any luck this morning's work might lead him on to the next.

The cathedral bell in the west tower rang and folk hurried to the cathedral for an evening Mass. Hubert was kneeling over drawings spread over the floor on top of the central tower, but when he heard the bell he stood and watched the scurrying people far below. His eyes narrowed. He saw a grey horse and knew whose it was. Edwin Pendock would not go to Mass while he had questions to ask.

"I'm going down," he called. "Carry on with your work. We mustn't lose the daylight."

He stepped out to the planks which floored the scaffolding and ran down the ladder at the side, before this Justice of the Peace could distract his men yet again.

He met Edwin halfway up. "You're out of breath," he said. "What now? Wouldn't it wait?"

"No, it would not. Does a man called Jude Cox work here?"

Hubert's face mottled with fury at the name. "No," he replied. "And I never want to see that idle, useless wretch again."

"Where is he now?" asked Edwin.

"I don't know and I don't care. In hell, with any luck."

"What has he done to make you so angry?"

"Nothing. That's the trouble. He came here when I was getting men together for this job. He was a mason all right. He came from Bromyard, so he said. If they're all like him there, I wonder there's a building standing. He never obeyed an order, he picked holes in what better men than him were proud to do, he got everyone else so angry I thought there'd be murder done. You can be glad that Christina was the first to fall off the tower. I'd have tipped master Jude Cox off myself if I hadn't got rid of him first. Sent him packing, I did, before he made any more trouble. And I've not seen him since, thank God."

"I see," said Edwin. "What would you say if I told you he was the source of the golden angel rumour?"

"I'd say I might have known it," Hubert answered. "That's just the sort of mischief he would make."

"Would you know him again?" Edwin asked.

"I reckon so," said Hubert. "His gargoyle face isn't easy to forget."

"And Abel, Will and Robin who found the body, which of them would you trust most?"

"Robin, I reckon. Or Abel. Perhaps Will. They're none of them bad lads."

"Did they know Jude Cox?"

"Aye. Like the rest of my men, they'll not forget him in a hurry."

Edwin made his mind up. This was just a possibility, but it would clear his mind a lot. "Could you spare them for an hour? And yourself? I want them to look at that body again and I want you with them."

Hubert felt his anger rising again. He thought he'd get rid of Edwin quickly this time. "Must we? Can't it wait?"

"I'm sorry, Hubert, it can't."

Hubert knew better than to say "No" to the justice and coroner. "Abel," he called. Abel, powdered white with lime from mortar and dust from hammered stone, appeared on the scaffold above. "Find Will and Robin and get yourselves down here. Quickly."

When all three were there, Edwin said, "We're off to St Peter's."

Joslin and Crispin rode their horses through Luke Thurn's lands. Crispin looked at the desolation round him and said. "I don't believe what I see."

They passed on a while without speaking. Then Crispin said, "What's happened? Luke may have treated me badly, but he was proud of this land, he loved it, it was cared for."

"Some of it is still cared for," said Joslin. He was looking beyond, to the neat cottages and the tenants' well-worked strips.

"Looking after themselves. Feathering their own nests," said Crispin bitterly. Then he softened and laughed. "Who can blame them?"

The land was deserted, just as when Edwin had been here a few hours earlier. "Why aren't they working?" said Joslin.

Crispin wasn't listening. He pointed to trees beyond the cottages. "Over there is the bailiff's house where I was born. You can't see it for the trees."

They came near Luke's house. "What's been going on here?" said Crispin. They stopped in front of the drawbridge. "Someone's built that bump on the end since I was last here," he said. "What is it?"

The stone boil on the end of a timber-framed, wattle and daub house – a dwarf's castle, a toy for a giant's baby – should have made them laugh. But it didn't. The battlemented top and the arrow slits round the floor below made it seem as if whoever built it thought he would have to defend it one day. House and keep together stared back at them, blank, expressionless, mysterious. And deserted as well?

"Is anyone in there?" Joslin said.

"Luke, I suppose. Madge and Christina, unless they're married." He seemed to have forgotten that Christina might be a dead nun.

"What will we do now?" asked Joslin.

"Go in, of course," said Crispin.

The body was lying in a coffin in front of the altar at St Peter's Church. Edwin looked for the priest. "Has anyone come to claim him?" he asked.

"Not a soul," the old priest answered. "Nobody seems to care."

"Perhaps these men will know who it is," said Edwin.

The priest lifted the coffin lid and raised the shroud. Edwin saw the ruined face again. Could *any-one* recognize it?

He spoke to Abel. "I remember you saying the face was known to you, but you couldn't tell where you saw it," he said.

"That's right, master Edwin," Abel replied.

"Can you tell me now?"

He waited for the answer. If Abel said, "I've no idea," and then denied it could be Jude Cox – and Hubert agreed – then he could call his work done. Jude murdered Christina. There weren't two people in Hereford suddenly fired with a wish to throw people off high places so Jude did the other killing as well. Once they caught Jude, they'd find out whose the second corpse was and why Christina was killed. Once Jude had paid the price for his crimes the whole business could be forgotten. But if Abel said, "Of course it is. I see it now," then his woes were only just beginning, for he would have to start all over again.

Abel looked hard at the swollen eyes, hideously smashed nose, squashed and bloody lips. "No," he said at last. "It's just a sort of way the face lies that makes me think of someone. I can't think who."

"What if I mentioned the name Jude Cox?"

"It could be," said Abel. He peered closely and finally said, "Then again, it might not. There's no way I can tell."

Edwin turned to Hubert. "Is it Jude Cox?"

"How can I say someone I always saw with a sneer, a curse or an evil grin on his face is anything like this poor thing? I wouldn't wish that on anybody, even Jude," Hubert replied. "I've no idea who it is."

"So it isn't Jude?"

"I never said that," Hubert replied. "It might be."

"You must have *some* idea." Edwin was almost pleading.

"I've said what I've said. It could be. But perhaps it isn't. No one could tell anything from that face."

"That's right, master Hubert," said Abel.

Wearily, Edwin called to the priest. "Nobody else is likely to claim the body," he said. "You can have him buried now. The city will pay. I'll be there, the only mourner."

Then he remembered the scar. He reached into the coffin and pulled away the shroud. "What about that?" he said, pointing to the man's right arm.

There was silence. Then Abel said, "It's Jude's. I saw it often enough when I was working beside him." He turned to Robin. "You remember it, don't you?"

Robin said, "Yes. He told me he got it in a knife fight years before. He said the one who gave it to him got paid back for it."

"So it is him," said Edwin.

"I reckon so," repled Hubert. "If these two are so sure."

"He's not the only one who ever got a cut on his arm," said Will. "Lots of us have. I have for one." He rolled his sleeve up. There, for all to see, was a scar not unlike the long gash on the dead man's.

"Never knew you'd been fighting with knives, Will," said Robin.

"No more I haven't," Will replied. "Someone dropped his trowel off the scaffolding. It hit me when I was below minding my own business."

"It's Jude," said Abel positively.

"Well, that's it, then," said Edwin. "I can bury him."

Hubert cleared his throat. "Seeing as it may be Jude and I knew him, I'd better be there as well," he said gruffly.

"And me," said Abel. "Because I know well it is him."

"So do I," said Robin.

"I'm not saying it's not," said Will. "But I won't say it is either."

"There's no one else going to come for him," said Edwin. "If we don't bury him quickly we'll have him stinking by evening."

"There's a grave dug," said the priest. "We'll do it now."

As Edwin watched the gravedigger hurl spadefuls of red earth on the coffin below him, he wondered whether he could say one part of this mystery was solved. Had he really found the murderer of Christina? If he had, now he must find the murderer of Jude. Kill one monster and another takes its place, he reflected bitterly.

As they scrambled into the ditch, squelched across the reeds, swung themselves over the fence and jumped down, Joslin and Crispin did not know Edwin had just done the same or that he had left the drawbridge down. Someone had raised it again.

Like Edwin, they hammered on the doors. "Luke," Crispin shouted. "Come on out. You'll have to face me in the end."

There was no answer.

"*Luke!*" Crispin shrieked. The house stared back like a dead man.

"He *must* be here," Crispin cried.

Like Edwin they looked round the outside, into the undercroft, through the windows. At each window, Crispin bellowed again. "Luke!"

They walked round three times. After the third, they stopped. Crispin was pale and very quiet.

"What are you thinking?" Joslin asked.

"What do you expect?" Crispin replied. His voice was bitter. "What homecoming is this? Why do I see only ruin and desolation?"

"You don't know yet," Joslin answered. "We must go on looking."

They scoured the courtyard, looking into stables and outbuildings. "Luke's not here. I know it," said Crispin bitterly. "Where's he gone? What has he done to his own house? This place was happy, full of life, when I was a boy. You can't know what seeing this makes me feel."

Joslin imagined homecomings of his own in the future: if they were like this then his quest was vain indeed. Then he saw the well. It reminded him of something. "Look at that," he said.

"Why?" Crispin answered. "It's only the well. The rope's broken. Nobody's been near it for years. What's happened to my lovely home?"

Joslin remembered what the well suggested. "You said the story of Gamelyn was your story," he said.

"That's right," Crispin replied."

"There's a well in that. Gamelyn is barred from his own house so he throws the gatekeeper down it. I remember the lines." He chanted:

"He soon caught the porter. Ignoring his groan
He seized his fat neck and shattered the bone
And threw the limp body straight down the well,
Seven fathoms deep so I've heard tell."

Crispin laughed. "Not every detail's the same," he said. "This is just a well which gave us good service once."

Joslin looked into the depths. "It hasn't run dry," he said. He saw the dark water and sinister glint that Edwin had seen. A rank smell climbed up. He stepped back "But I wouldn't drink from it," he added.

"No one has," said Crispin. "Not for a long time. . ."

"That well worries me," said Joslin.

Crispin didn't listen. "I'm getting inside the house," he announced.

"We'll never break those doors down," said Joslin.

"We don't need to." Crispin was looking at a mullioned window with small panes of cloudy, rough glass. "We'll break this. Trust me."

Joslin looked doubtful.

"It's my home," said Crispin. "I'll do what I like."

He went back to the well. The mortar on the wall round it was loose. He heaved at a stone on the top and pulled it off. Then he smashed it through the window. There was a crash: the window was left with a jagged hole and a twisted network of lead, like petrified grey worms. He pushed them back until there was a gap. He hoisted himself up and disappeared through it like a monstrous owl into its nest.

Joslin hesitated and then followed. They were in a small room. Joslin guessed it was the solar. Crispin confirmed it.

"Luke's solar, and my father's before him. I remember my father in here," he said, "It was where he came for solitude. I guess it gave him good thoughts of what it was like to find he was a gentleman."

Joslin noticed a sardonic note. "Isn't what we're doing to make sure you're a gentleman yourself?" he asked. The word "gentleman" didn't quite fit Crispin the minstrel, outlaw, righter of wrongs.

"When I get back what's rightfully mine I'll be a gentleman and yeoman different from most the folk have known," Crispin said firmly.

"I know," Joslin answered. He looked round. There was an oak settle and a table. Everything was thick with dust. Crispin stood still for a long time, thinking his own thoughts.

At last, he spoke. "Strange," he said. "This room is smaller than I remember." He looked round, puzzled. Then he said, "It's the years playing tricks." He paused again: then, "We're the first in here for a long time. *Where is Luke?*"

He crossed to a door in the corner. It opened on the latch. He stepped out and Joslin followed. They were in the hall. The ceiling was high, with overarching oak roofbeams. A long table stretched down the middle, with benches either side and a carved chair at each end. At the other end of the hall was a huge fireplace. But there were no tapestries, coats of arms, trappings of power and riches here. Instead, spiders' webs, grey dust like dirty snow, more signs of desertion.

"Empty. Luke's abandoned it. The place is mine for the taking," said Crispin.

"Has he?" Joslin replied. Something worried him – a pricking of the thumbs, coldness in his stomach. "Do you think we're really alone?"

"What sort of talk is that? Of course we're alone. Look around you. Nothing moves except mice, rats and bats."

"How do we get in the tower?" said Joslin.

"We'll find a door," said Crispin and led into the kitchen, where no fire had been lit for many a day, and up narrow stairways. The story was the same – dust and cobwebs. "No Luke, no Madge, no Christina," said Crispin.

"No door either," said Joslin.

"I don't know where to look," Crispin replied. "That pathetic poor man's fortress is new." His voice was strident with frustration.

"Then we'll keep trying," said Joslin.

At last they found a door, deep in the far corner of the hall behind the fireplace. It was strong, without any latch or bolt. "It must be barred on the other side," said Joslin. "We'd need a battering ram."

They pulled at it, pummelled it, then stepped back. "This is no good," Crispin groaned.

"Someone doesn't want us in there," said Joslin.

"There has to be a better way than this," said Crispin. "When I'm master here, I'll either open that fool's work up properly or knock it down. As it is, it's no use to anyone."

"Let's look outside," said Joslin.

The fresh air was a relief. Crispin calmed down in the sunshine. They walked round the tower. "We'd need ropes and tackle to climb it," said Joslin. He remembered Stovenham castle and his terrified scramble down the barbizon. At least there were hand and footholds in those flint and mortar walls. This tower was built of blocks of stone, too smooth to climb like that. "Even if we could climb it, we'd have to go to the top. The arrow slits are too narrow to get through," he said.

"What a waste of stone that tower is," said Crispin disgustedly.

"We won't know it's empty until we've been inside," Joslin replied.

Crispin stood back and looked at it. "Those battlements are only fit for children's games," he said. "Does someone expect an army of midgets?" He turned away. "I've seen enough. We'll go."

"Then we've wasted a day. We must do *something*," said Joslin.

"Such as?" asked Crispin derisively.

"If there were people working that land over there," Joslin replied, "they would know something."

"Some of the men who should be there were my friends in the bad days," said Crispin. "But then, some weren't. Still, why talk about them? Friends or enemies, they aren't there now."

Joslin was looking towards where the cottages stood amid the neat, well-worked land. An old man had appeared, leaning on a hoe and watching them intently. "Yes they are," he said.

They approached the cottages, ten of them, almost a tiny village. They skirted land where thin wheat showed and picked their way between cowpats. The old man leaning on his hoe cried, "I know you. Master Crispin, I thought you were dead."

"I'm far from dead, Coll," Crispin replied. "But it seems the rest of my family must be."

Others heard them. People appeared from the cottages as if they had been waiting – men, aproned wives, youths, dirty children and yapping, yellow-eyed dogs sniffing suspiciously. Crispin surveyed them. "So Luke's home isn't deserted," he said. "It's been many years, but I think I recognize most of you." He looked round, then said, "Where's Hawkin?"

A burly, fair-haired man was approaching, walking fast. "I'm here, Crispin," he shouted.

Joslin said quietly, "Crispin, if you know them so well, why didn't they come to greet us before? They're not frightened, are they?"

Crispin nudged him sharply with his elbow. "Quiet," he whispered. Joslin followed his gaze. One man avoided Crispin's eyes – a thin, dark man who looked as if he wanted no part of this reunion.

Crispin spoke. "I've come back. Some of you know why I left."

"Now you're here to claim what's yours," said Hawkin.

"Yes. At last." Crispin stopped, to see what the reaction was.

Very little. They looked back stonily. Even Hawkin said nothing. The thin man turned and fixed Crispin with a hostile glare. Crispin glared back. "So you're still here are you, Lud?" he said.

The man did not answer. He looked away again.

"What's been happening?" Crispin said. "Where's my family?"

Old Coll cleared his throat. "I'm sorry, Crispin," he said, "but what's gone on in that house is a mystery to us."

"Surely you know why that mad tower was built?" Crispin insisted.

More silence. Then the man Crispin called Lud looked Crispin full in the face. "We're looking at the reason," he said.

"You mean Luke was so afeared of his little brother that he turned his home into a castle to keep him out?" Crispin scoffed. He turned to the man he called Hawkin. "We were good friends once," he said. "Haven't you anything to say to me?"

Hawkin looked as if he wanted to speak, but daren't.

"It's been a poor homecoming," said Crispin disgustedly. "I thought you'd still be my friends, but you're not worth talking to."

There was an uneasy quiet: some could not help a

fleeting glance at Lud. Crispin turned his back on tenants and cottages and headed for his horse. Joslin followed. "They're frightened," he said. "You can see it in their eyes. I think it's all they could manage to come out and see you. I don't think Lud wanted them to."

"I thought better of Hawkin," Crispin answered.

They untied the horses and rode away. But hardly had they turned on to the road back to Hereford than they heard running footsteps and a voice. "Crispin! Wait a moment!" It was Hawkin. He caught up, panting, and gasped, "Crispin, there's a lot I couldn't say to you."

"Because of Lud?" asked Joslin.

"Aye," said Hawkin. "We saw you coming this morning. Lud made us stay out of sight. Just like he did when the man from Hereford came sniffing round earlier. We live like mice behind the wainscot here. I managed to slip out for a moment: Lud doesn't know I've gone. There'll be hell to pay if he finds out."

"I don't understand why Lud has such a hold over you," said Crispin. "What is he, but one man? And a coward at that."

"One man?" Hawkin replied. "I wish only one man kept us down."

"Tell me what you know, Hawkin," said Crispin.

"Let's get off the road where we won't be seen," Hawkin replied.

Crispin and Joslin dismounted and Hawkin led them into a clump of trees.

"Well?" said Crispin. "First, where's Luke?"

"I don't know," said Hawkin. "I think he may be with Madge."

"Madge? Where's she now?"

"Madge is married. A Welshman from the other

side of the hills. Gwilym, his name is. Luke was delighted with the match. Gwilym owns a manor, wide lands and many sheep. And much else besides. He's a great man on his side of the border and a good catch for the Thurns."

"Why do you only *think* Luke's with Madge?" asked Joslin.

"Because we only have Lud's word for it."

"Why should Lud know and nobody else?" Joslin asked this though he had a good idea why already. Crispin confirmed it. "Lud was always Luke's own creature," he said. "Lud is a spy. He tells Luke everything the tenants say and think. It was so before I left and it seems nothing has changed. I'm surprised Lud hasn't had a knife in the back and a bed in a ditch by now. Luke needed Lud. He'd heard rumours of peasants rising up and throwing over their masters. Now he was a master himself, he wanted none of that here." He laughed. "Time was when the boot was on the other foot."

"You can well say that," said Hawkin. "Many of the older ones sigh for the days of your father."

Joslin was surprised that Crispin hadn't asked the obvious question. So he asked it. "What about Christina?" he said.

Hawkin looked away. "As to Christina, I couldn't say," he said.

"Could she be in St Katherine's nunnery?" Joslin asked.

"She could," Hawkin answered

"So close and yet you don't know?" cried Crispin.

"Crispin, we're prisoners here. We know nothing of the world outside," Hawkin answered. "It's not just Lud."

"What about Christina?" Crispin asked, his voice hard with anger.

"If she's not in Wales with Luke she could be in the nunnery. She could be in London. She could be with the Angel Gabriel."

Crispin suddenly roared in frustration. "Why does nobody know anything round here?"

"Because there's nothing to know except what's deep in the past. One day about five years ago, Madge was married to Gwylim and afterwards set off for Wales. Luke set her up with a good dowry and bought fine clothes for her journey. We were surprised that Luke's men didn't go with her, but he seemed to know what he wanted. Gwylim took her over the hills to Wales with his own men. That's the last we saw of her. A month later, Luke prepared for a journey himself. He said he was visiting Madge and would only take his steward. He told us not to question his word or make enquiries if he was not back soon. He said Christina would look after the house."

"And that was the last you saw of my brother?" said Crispin. "I can't believe you let things slide like that."

"No," said Hawkin. "He came back a month later. He was alone: the steward wasn't with him. We've not seen the steward since. We could not believe what happened next."

"What was it?" said Crispin impatiently.

"Luke brought masons and builders to the house from miles around – hardly any local men. He brought in piles of stone as well, and the tower was started. One day when Lud wasn't looking, I dared to approach Luke and ask what this fortress was for. 'I have a vengeful brother,' he said. In less than a year the tower was finished. Soon afterwards Lud spoke to us. 'Our master has gone on another journey.' 'Why couldn't he tell us himself?' I said. 'Because he trusts me,' said Lud. We've not seen Luke since."

"And Christina?" asked Crispin quietly.

"Nor her," said Hawkin.

Crispin's voice was raised in sheer disbelief. "You mean you've seen nothing of either of them?"

"The night before Lud told us they had gone," said Hawkin, "we heard shouts, as if a fight was going on. There were flaring torches: the house looked as if it were alight. We gathered outside the cottages. 'We must go,' I said. 'Perhaps Luke needs help.' But Lud forbade it. 'Not at all,' he said. They're preparing for their journey. Luke is going back to Wales and taking Christina with him. They'll be gone before dawn. It's Luke's express wish that they aren't interrupted.' I remember Coll saying, 'That's a terrible noise for two people getting ready.' Lud answered, 'They have a lot to do.' Next morning the house was empty. They must have left before dawn. That was more than three years ago: we've expected them back every day ever since."

"But why don't you keep the house in good order?" said Joslin.

"It's Luke's command. We must not go there."

"I expect Lud told you that," said Crispin sarcastically.

"Crispin," Hawkin answered. "It's all right for you. You're Luke's brother and can say what you like to Lud. But to us, Lud speaks with Luke's voice. We daren't question him."

Crispin swore suddenly and violently. "The man's playing a crooked game," he shouted. "And I'll find out what it is."

"Are you sure Christina is with Luke?" asked Joslin.

"So Lud says," said Hawkin. "All I know is that if she's in St Katherine's like you asked, there's no chance Luke's with her. Why do you say that anyway?"

Joslin told them of the nun with the same name thrown from the tower. "Didn't you hear?" he asked.

"We hear about nothing that happens outside," said Hawkin.

"So you didn't hear that this dead nun's hair was pure white?"

"Then it's not Christina," said Hawkin. "Her's was black and shining. It was so the last time I saw her, before they left in the night."

"What do you make of it all, Hawkin?" Crispin said.

"I make nothing," said Hawkin stiffly. "I only say what I know."

"And what you've been told by a man I don't trust an inch," Crispin replied. "If you haven't questioned what Lud said, you're not the man I took you for."

There was a battle of wills going on: Crispin willing Hawkin to say more and Hawkin willing himself to dare to. At last, Hawkin said, "Of course I don't believe it. There's far more gone on than what Lud says. But I'm sure the tower is nothing to do with you. I believe Luke used you as a good excuse."

"So what other reason could there be?" Crispin asked.

Hawkin looked fixedly at the ground. "The soil round here must be mighty interesting," Crispin burst out. "I've never seen people spend so much time studying it."

They were getting nowhere. Then Joslin asked,

"Hawkin, what was in the marriage settlement beween Gwylim and Madge?"

Hawkin looked almost relieved. "All I know is that Luke made sure Madge's dowry was a good one worth having and fit to unite two notable families. As for Gwylim. . ." he paused.

"Yes?" said Joslin.

"He had a possession beyond price, made of pure gold."

"What was it?" Crispin asked. "A ring? A crown? A chalice?"

"None of those. It was an angel."

Hawkin watched Crispin and his companion ride away together. He waited a moment, then pushed his way through the trees to the road.

Without warning, a hard hand roughly stopped his mouth, an arm clamped his own arms behind him. A voice hissed in his ear.

"Never think nobody can hear you, Hawkin. Nowhere is safe from eavesdroppers, even lonely woods by empty roads. Long ears listen at every corner. It's amazing what they can pick up. You were ordered never to tell anybody what happened on Thurn lands. Yet you've told the last person who should know. That's bad enough. But you've done far, far worse than that. You've put the idea of golden angels in his head. That was the most foolish thing you ever did in your whole life."

Hawkin struggled, but he was in the grip of someone far stronger.

"And not only the most foolish," the voice continued.

Hawkin tried to bite the hand gagging him so he could cry for help.

"But the last as well," said the voice.

For the briefest instant Hawkin was well aware of a knife at his throat, but he knew nothing else after that, except the same voice. "A pity there's no high place to send you to your death from. Much more to our taste. But this will have to do. I'm sorry about that."

Thus Hawkin was left, dead and alone, in a thicket of rowan trees which must have grown used to acting as a morgue for the newly murdered.

17

Back at the inn, Crispin was gloomy. "I'm further from my rights now than if I'd stayed an outlaw in the Forest of Arden," he said.

"But you learned a lot today," replied Joslin. "You heard that Madge is set up in comfort for the rest of her life and that Luke went on a journey to see her. When he comes back, you can sort out your differences like any brothers would."

"That's what you really think, is it?" said Crispin.

He wouldn't lie to Crispin. "No, it's not. I expect it's what Lud wants us to believe. But I doubt if it's the truth."

There was silence. Then Crispin said, "What about Christina?"

"I don't think she went to Wales. I believe the murdered nun was your sister," Joslin replied. "I also believe that the answer to her murder may be in Luke's house."

"Why should you think that? asked Crispin.

"Because Coll said a man from Hereford came looking early this morning. We're not the only ones looking for Christina's killer."

115

"Why does that dead nun have to be my sister? Hawkin said Christina's hair was black and shining on the last day he saw her before they were supposed to leave. The nun's was white."

"I know," Joslin replied. "But Hawkin also said there was disturbance that night. Even old Coll said, 'That's a lot of noise from people who are only getting ready.' There's only Lud's word they set off on a journey and he terrorizes anyone who thinks otherwise."

"I don't see what you're getting at," said Crispin.

"You *must* do," said Joslin. "I believe something bad happened that night – so bad that Christina ran out of the house and didn't stop until she reached the only place she could think of where she would find shelter and safety. St Katherine's nunnery."

Crispin thought about this. "Even if you're right," he answered, "it doesn't tell me why her hair should be white."

"It could. What if the things she saw that night struck such sheer terror into her that her hair turned white with shock?"

The silence at Edwin's dinner table could be cut with a knife. Wife, family, servants – all saw his mood and dared not speak. When the last morsel was cleared away, Edwin retired to his solar. Here, he paced up and down trying to think of connections, different paths to take, new people to speak to.

Nothing. A blank.

He sat in his carved wooden chair and spoke, though there was nobody to hear him. "Hereford is cursed," he groaned. "I need a stroke of fortune. I need a sign from God to show the curse will be lifted."

* * *

"I want to talk to Arthur again," said Joslin.

"Why? What has he got except a mixed-up head?" Crispin replied.

"He knows more than he thinks. The keys to this business are in the cathedral as much as they are at Luke's. He may have them."

"All right." Crispin unwillingly stood up. "How will you find him?"

"We'll go to St Ethelbert's and look."

By the time they came back to the cathedral, the city was dark and the nave even darker except for lit candles. There were few people inside. There was no sign of Arthur.

"Now what shall we do?" said Crispin.

"Try the side chapels," Joslin replied.

But wherever they looked, in every chapel, in the chamber where the Mappa Mundi stood in its wooden case, in the press of pilgrims at St Thomas Cantilupe's shrine, there was no sign of Arthur. "Give up," said Crispin. "He won't tell us anything, anyway."

They were back in the nave. "We may as well. . ." Crispin began. Suddenly they were nearly knocked down by three men carrying a long ladder down the nave towards the west door. "Watch where you're going," Crispin shouted. His voice echoed round the high nave. Pilgrims looked round at him, shocked.

"You watch out yourself," retorted the man at the front end.

"Don't be so hasty, Will," said the man halfway along. "If I had my way, this ladder wouldn't ever be brought here again, if it's true that poor nun was pushed up it before she was cast down to her death."

"Well, you can be sure it will be, Abel," said the

117

man at the front. "If Hubert thinks we need ladders inside as well as out, he'll have them."

Crispin stopped in his tracks. "Is that true?" he asked. "Is this really the ladder she was taken up to her death?"

"So Master Edwin thinks," said Abel. "And he should know."

"So does Hubert. Don't forget that," said Will.

"Who are Edwin and Hubert," asked Joslin.

"Edwin Pendock is Justice of the Peace and coroner," said Abel. "He lives in Bridge Street. He's the one charged with finding out who did these terrible murders. Hubert Fennel's our master."

"And you saw this Christina?" asked Crispin.

"For the whole day," said the man at the back end of the ladder. "We lifted her on to our cart and bore her off to St Katherine's where she belongs. Nobody saw her more than us."

"Except the poor priest who found her," said Abel. "Don't forget him, Robin. He was in a bad way about it."

"Well, we found the other body in the rowan trees," said Robin. "If that priest is in a bad way because he found a body, then so are we."

"Tell me," said Crispin. "About this Christina. Is it true her hair was white?"

"As snow," said Will.

"As a bride's gown," said Abel.

"As a bishop's bed sheets," said Robin.

"For all she was so young," said Will.

"What a waste," said Abel. "She was a fair maid lost to men in that nunnery. That would turn anyone's hair white, I should think."

They seemed to think this was a chance of a rest

and a good talk. They put the ladder on the floor and stood round the minstrels in a companionable group.

"But with hair like that, she couldn't have been as young as you think," Crispin insisted.

"That we can't tell you," said Robin. "All I can say is that she looked a young girl to me."

The only sounds in the nave were shuffling pilgrims and kneeling, muttering worshippers. Then Joslin said, "Do you take the ladder out of the cathedral every night?"

"Aye," said Will. "We do that. Hubert wants to see everything we have that could be stolen and sold under lock and key."

"Then why was it here on the night the nun died?" Joslin asked.

"That's a good question," said Abel.

"Because someone moved it, that's why," said Robin. "When he brought it back he didn't leave it quite in the right place. Next morning, Hubert could see it had been shifted."

"He would," said Will.

"But it must have still been under lock and key," said Joslin.

"Yes," said Abel. "It was."

"So whoever took it must have had a key," said Crispin.

"Well, it weren't one of us masons," said Will. "So don't you go thinking it, whoever you are."

"If he didn't have his own key he must have had some way of getting one," said Joslin. "If he can steal ladders, he can steal keys. Do priests have keys?" It would make things very bleak for Arthur in his anguish if they did.

"Them?" scoffed Robin. "They're the last people Hubert would trust with them."

Joslin looked up at the roof, where the weak candlelight below made it disappear into mysterious, pitch darkness. "What are you building in here anyway?" he said.

"I'll tell you what," said Will. "You've got honest faces, the two of you. So since you're so interested, and as long as you didn't steal the ladder yourselves and throw the poor girl off, you can come with us for a pot of ale in the tavern opposite, and as long as you buy it we'll tell you everything you want to know."

"That is if we know it ourselves," said Abel.

They took up their places on the ladder, heaved it up and resumed their journey. Joslin and Crispin followed them out round the cathedral's bulky sides and watched them slide it into the tool store with the rest of the masons' implements, helped by the watchman.

"Who's that little runt?" said Crispin when they had finished.

"Him?" said Will. "Ulf. Take no notice."

The minstrels and masons had sat for hours drinking first ale, then cider. By the time they left, Crispin and Joslin had learnt everything the masons could tell them about the murders. When Crispin heard the second body was found right opposite Luke's place, he turned pale.

"Someone had really beaten his face in," said Will cheerfully. "You've never seen such a mess. We reckon it might be that Jude Cox. But you couldn't recognize a thing on that face."

When Abel had explained who Jude Cox was, Joslin

asked, "Did many masons from here work on the tower at Luke Thurn's place?"

"That was a few years back," said Robin disgustedly. "Work on the cathedral hadn't started. There weren't any masons' jobs in Hereford."

"Yet none of us worked on that tower," said Will.

"He got his masons from anywhere but Hereford," said Abel.

"Might this Jude Cox have worked there?" Joslin asked.

"He might and he might not," said Robin. "He never said."

"All I know is he was supposed to come from Bromyard," said Will.

"So does my cousin and he's never heard of him," said Abel.

There was no more to ask about Jude Cox. Crispin's face was pale, as if every new thing he heard struck a new blow. Another murder and the body left outside his own brother's place – not pleasant to hear after everything else today. Joslin felt he should change the subject. "What's the work at the cathedral?" he asked.

"The central tower," said Abel.

"It was started years ago. How long would it be, Robin?" said Will.

"Near on fifty years, I reckon," said Robin. "My father was an apprentice when they started work. I don't think this King Edward was on the throne then."

"But the work stopped when the plague came, for all it was nearly finished," said Abel.

"It would have started again before this, but the plague came a second time to Hereford, as bad as the first," said Robin.

"It's only now, when there's enough masons and

enough money to do it that we're about finishing it," said Will.

"It will be wonderful," said Abel.

"It is now," said Robin. "We're proud of what we've done."

"Even though there won't be no golden angel at the top," said Abel.

Crispin roused himself from his silence. "Why should we think there would be?" he said.

"Didn't you hear the rumour?" asked Will.

"We've only just come here," said Joslin. "How could we?"

"Well, I'll tell you," said Robin. "Somebody spread some cock and bull tale about putting this angel at the top of the tower. It'd be bright gold and when the sun shone you'd be able to see it for miles around."

"Only there won't be no angel," said Will. "There never was."

"We've had to spend a lot of time trying to make people believe that," said Robin. "I wish I knew where the story came from. It's put us to such bother these last few weeks."

"Edwin reckons Jude started it," said Will. "Something to do with what he found when he went to St Katherine's. I didn't quite understand that bit."

"Hubert thinks so too," said Abel.

"Well, if we hear it, we'll know not to believe it," said Crispin.

Soon after, they all left and Joslin and Crispin returned to their own inn. Joslin looked back at the cathedral's huge east tower and the even bigger central tower beyond it, and thought that to be a master mason and carry such a building in your head before seeing it rise up in front of you, must be a great thing indeed.

As they entered the inn, Joslin said, "That's twice we've heard about golden angels today."

"I know," said Crispin. "I wish I'd heard neither."

"So what next?" said Crispin.

"We need help," Joslin replied.

"Who from?"

"Remember what the masons said? There's a coroner investigating the whole business."

"What was his name? How do we find him?"

"Edwin something. They said he lives in Bridge Street."

Crispin groaned. "What new bed of serpents have we landed in? It seems Christina's foully murdered. I have to believe that now. Another man's found dead outside my own house. Luke has disappeared. Only my elder sister is left and she's far away. How many more will there be?"

"And that strange rumour about an angel of gold," said Joslin.

"No, I'm not having that," Crispin replied. "What connection can there be between a silly rumour that the masons say is completely untrue and something my sister's husband in Wales possesses?"

"Crispin," Joslin replied. "I think this golden angel

rumour matters. There's something strange about it."

Crispin merely groaned again.

"We'll go to Bridge Street and see the coroner," said Joslin.

Arthur pulled his white nightshirt on, tried to make himself comfortable in his bed and prayed for sleep to come quickly. His eyes stung and his mind raced with feverish thoughts. He would not sleep tonight. Nobody could expect sleep in such a state as his. He groaned as he imagined the night of terror that awaited him in the recesses of his mind.

Then, without warning, a black, smothering slumber took him. He fell back on his bed, arms and legs spread out at grotesque angles.

When there was a knock at the door of the solar and news that two minstrels wanted to see him, Edwin's first thought was that songs were the last thing he needed.

"They say they have urgent business about the job you're doing," said the servant.

"Send them in," Edwin said. He had a short way with time-wasters.

One was tall with a square jaw which reminded him somehow of an axe blade; the other was young and slim, with long dark hair. Could he be foreign? What urgent business could strangers have about Hereford murders? But as soon as the tall one spoke, Edwin knew this must be the sign, the stroke of Providence, that he had prayed for.

"I am Crispin Thurn, brother of Luke Thurn. He dispossessed me of my rights many years ago and now I have come to claim them."

"Yes," said Edwin. Now he recognized them. These were the two who entered Hereford yesterday as he brought the body back.

"But that is not why I am here tonight. I believe my sister Christina has been murdered."

It *was* the sign. Edwin breathed his thanks, resolved to be a better man and cooperate with the Church, even when the dean and bishop annoyed him. To Crispin he said, "Why should you think that?"

Crispin told his story. "I remember hearing about it at the time," Edwin murmured. Crispin said how he had vowed to come back one day and claim his inheritance and was now returned with his good friend Joslin de Lay. Then he told of all that had happened since they came to Hereford. Finally, Crispin stopped. "That's all we know," he said.

For the first time, the young minstrel Crispin called Joslin de Lay spoke. Edwin knew at once that this man was neither Welsh nor English. "Crispin, it's not all we know," he said. "You said it wasn't Christina dead when you heard the nun had white hair. But I believe she saw something which frightened her so much her hair turned white. And you've forgotten what Hawkin said about Gwylim's golden angel."

"As to the nun's white hair, I must agree with you, which is all the more reason for finding out what happened," Edwin replied. "As to the golden angel – it is strange." But he did not tell these two about his encounter with Mildred and Rosette. That would follow when he was more sure of them. They must tell him more before he would be fully open. "What do you know about the golden angel?"

"Nothing," said Crispin. "Hawkin merely said that

Gwylim possessed a golden angel which was priceless."

"But rumours about golden angels have been sweeping Hereford lately," said Joslin. "So the masons told us. That's too many rumours about the same thing to ignore."

Edwin looked closely at the young foreign minstrel. The man had a fast brain: he should either be taken notice of or watched carefully. "You may be right," he said. "Let me get this clear. If this golden angel exists, it's a treasured possession of Gwylim from Wales, the husband of your elder sister Madge. And Christina is Madge's younger sister and therefore Gwylim's sister-in-law. Am I right?"

"You are," said Crispin.

"And how did Christina feel about Gwylim and Madge? Was she jealous or happy for them? Did she love Gwylim secretly herself?"

"How in God's name am I supposed to know?" cried Crispin. "I've been away for years. Until today I'd never heard of this Gwylim. But I'll say this. If dear, gentle Christina ever had a jealous thought in her head, then she changed mightily after I left." He stopped and his eyes narrowed suspiciously. "Why should you ask, anyway?"

Edwin decided to take the chance. "What would you say to this?" he said. "The masons told you about Jude Cox. Well, I have more to say. Jude Cox came to work at St Katherine's nunnery. He told your sister Christina that he knew about a golden angel which was placed 'where Hereford touches Heaven'. He seemed to be saying that he alone was responsible for putting it there. Where could that be but the top of St Ethelbert's tower? What do you make of that, Crispin Thurn?"

"I say you should seize this Jude Cox and and beat the full truth out of him, " Crispin replied. "He lured my poor, dear, trusting sister to her death." His face was dark with anger. "He's the man. If we find him, we avenge Christina."

"I wish it were so easy," said Edwin, "I'm sure the dead man in the rowan thicket was Jude Cox. The face is so badly disfigured it could be anyone. I took Hubert, Abel, Will and Robin to see the body. Abel and Robin are sure it's Jude, but only because of a scar on his arm. Will doesn't believe it. I think Jude, too, may have been thrown from a tower. But it can't be St Ethelbert's tower." He stopped and looked at their intent faces. Neither minstrel answered him.

He continued. "If the dead man is Jude Cox and he killed Christina, then someone in turn killed him the same way. So where are we now? And why was the body left there by the roadway?"

"The only connection between this Jude Cox and precious objects owned by Gwylim of Wales is that he might have helped build Luke's tower," said Crispin.

"If Jude was thrown from a tower," said Joslin, "where was it?"

"I don't know," Edwin answered cautiously. *Let them supply the answer*, he thought.

"Isn't it obvious?" said Joslin. "It can't be another tower in Hereford. Nobody saw the body fall or found it on the ground. It would have to be carried away with nobody seeing. The body was found in rowan trees. We talked to Hawkin in the same trees. The nearest tower to them has to be Luke's castle keep."

"Are you saying all these events started from my own home?" said Crispin. "No, I'll not have that."

"I wish I could say that all this evil comes from that

one place," Edwin said. "It would make the business much clearer."

"I can't bear the thought that my brother is behind it," said Crispin. "He treated me badly, but I won't believe he plotted the murder of his own sister."

Edwin spoke slowly now, choosing his words carefully. "From now on we must work together. But that doesn't mean we have to *be* together. I think we'll be of more use to each other if we carry on our own ways, knowing what the other knows and meeting at the end of the day to tell each other what we've found."

Crispin looked at him suspiciously. "Don't you trust us?" he said.

"Of course I do," Edwin replied. "I mean we'll be in two places at the same time, find out twice the information and work twice as fast."

"I see," said Crispin. But his eyes were suspicious still.

"There's something else," said Edwin. "Agatha, prioress of St Katherine's, rode out of her nunnery yesterday. Her horse came back alone, but she has not been seen since. Make what you like of that."

"It must be to do with Christina," said Joslin.

"I know," Edwin replied.

"So what shall we do tomorrow?" asked Joslin.

"I've made no plans," Edwin replied. "I was going to sleep on it."

There seemed no more to say. Soon, the minstrels took their leave.

Outside, Crispin was angry. "I'm right," he said. "He doesn't trust us. He thinks we're playing some doubtful game of our own."

"Well, aren't we?" said Joslin.

"That's not how I see it," said Crispin and strode

towards the inn.

After they had gone, Edwin sat back in his carved chair and felt less confused than for the last two days. Then he thought of Agatha's disappearance. Everything which had happened today suggested where Agatha might have gone. If some ruthless demon hid in that tower of Luke Thurn's giving orders for murder to be done, might Agatha be the next victim? Or was she one already?

He went over everything that the minstrels had said. He remembered a question he had asked which neither took up. It was about the body. "*Why was the body left there by the roadway?*"

Well, why? Anyone could see it when Arthur and the masons left St Katherine's. But when they came back for the body, it was hidden: presumably nobody would have seen it again until then. As they brought it into Hereford on the cart, Crispin and Joslin must have been quite close behind them.

What if they had reached the rowan trees first and found it? What if Crispin had found such a disfigured sight as a welcome to his own brother's house? What message would he have taken? Could it be that some-one knew they were coming. That body would have said, clearly as if a notice had been nailed to a tree, *Go away, Crispin, or this will happen to you.*

No, how could it? The body was placed there hours before they passed by. Why, he, Arthur and the masons had nearly reached Hereford with it before the minstrels passed them – and they were moving much quicker.

So why was it there? *Why? Why? Why?*

"I wish," said Joslin, "that we could have spoken to Arthur tonight."

Crispin laughed. "We've got more from three simple masons than from any over-educated priest," he said. "Not to mention the coroner."

"I know," Joslin replied. "Even so. . ."

"Are you thinking of going back to the cathedral?" said Crispin. He looked keenly at Joslin. "You are, aren't you?"

"Yes, I am. There are Masses at night in English cathedrals, aren't there? He'll be there and I'm going whether you like it or not. It's important."

Crispin shrugged his shoulders. "Then go if you must," he said. "It's near midnight now. If you end up in the cells don't expect me to get you out."

"That's the least of our worries," Joslin answered.

The street outside was deserted. Soon the cathedral stood before him, dark, with a slight candle glimmer through the great west window. He stood outside the west door and looked round. Had anybody seen him? There was no movement anywhere except for the white, ghostly shapes of owls drifting through the air on silent wings, no sound except for their occasional mournful cries. Then he saw another owl, much larger – in fact huge, monstrous - skimming the ground.

Not, it was not an owl. What was it? A ghost? The white shape approached slowly, but inexorably.

It was no ghost. It was a man. Even in the darkness, he could make out who it was. "Arthur," Joslin called.

Arthur walked on, like a puppet. As he came near, Joslin saw his eyes, wide open, glittering and yet, Joslin knew well, seeing nothing.

Arthur was doing what he had feared most. He was walking in his sleep. Once that was happening, who could tell what else he might do?

Edwin was awake, mulling over what the two minstrels told him. Did he trust them? He couldn't say. The young one, the foreigner, was right when he said they should work together. But the other, Luke Thurn's brother, seemed a surly devil. After being disinherited and returning home to find his sister dead and his brother missing, who could blame him? It was surely right that they should work separately, whether he trusted them or not. Yes, what they had said certainly added to what he already knew, but somehow his new knowledge made the puzzle even harder. What could he do next? Go to Bromyard and ask about Jude Cox? That would waste a whole day if, as he was sure, he would find nobody claiming to know the elusive mason.

His wife beside him woke and whispered. "Are you still awake, Edwin? You have too much on your mind. Go to sleep."

"I wish I could," he muttered and vainly closed his eyes yet again.

"I keep thinking of that poor prioress, gone who knows where," said his wife drowsily.

Her level breathing told him she had at once gone easily back to sleep. Edwin stayed awake. He looked at the ceiling. It was as if his wife had told him what to do. "Poor Agatha." Yes, he must attend to her disappearance next.

How should he do it? It was tempting to accept what the minstrels said and go straight to Thurn's stunted castle. Should he call on them in the morning? Then all three could go and Crispin Thurn would be a proper guide as well as a warrant for being inside the place.

No, that wouldn't do. He could not go to Thurn's assuming Agatha was there. Now he knew more about Christina, he must go back to St Katherine's. He must speak to old Sister Joan, who looked after Agatha's pony. Perhaps she could remember something Agatha said. He was almost certain that Christina was Luke Thurn's sister, in spite of her white hair. He'd speak to Freya, the manciple, who must know almost as much about the nunnery as Agatha did and might have some idea of where the nuns came from. In the light of what Crispin Thurn had said, he might also ask Mildred and Rosette to tell him their story again.

"Right," he said aloud. "Have I made up my mind about that?" The answer was "Yes," so he closed his eyes and slept at once.

Joslin followed Arthur into the nave. Inside, Arthur stopped and looked round. Joslin remained still.

Perhaps Arthur might wake up. It might be disastrous if he saw him.

He didn't. Arthur slowly swivelled his head round again so it looked straight ahead. Then he continued his unearthly, tranced progress. Joslin followed just behind.

If other people were in the cathedral they must be locked in their thoughts and devotions. Arthur kept on to the crossing. Here, he stopped. He looked upwards. Even though his eyes seemed to focus on something high above, Joslin knew he still saw nothing.

He silently crept close to the unconscious priest. He knew that to wake him suddenly might be dangerous. But perhaps he could—

There was a sudden gasp. Then there was a muffled cry of distress. "No. Not again."

Joslin recoiled. But he was sure he hadn't woken him. Something else, far more important to Arthur, had done that. What could it be? Arthur's eyes were blinking now: his face was horror-stricken. But there had been no sudden sound, nothing except the familar crossing, pillars and scaffolding. Could it be that what had woken Arthur was *the place he had come to*? This was where the battle against his guilt, and for his soul, would take place.

Joslin took a step back, watched and waited. Arthur still looked up, his lips moving silently. Then he dropped to his knees and Joslin heard him gabbling furiously. These prayers were desperate.

Now was the time. Joslin moved up to him and knelt by his side. "The prayers will be answered," he said. "They will."

Arthur started, then turned to Joslin. His face was

featureless in the dark, but his eyes still glittered. He seemed to have made an easy transition back into conscious life. "I found myself here last night and I don't know how I got here. I'm here again tonight. What's happening to me?"

"You were sleepwalking," said Joslin gently.

"Am I to walk here every night until I die?" cried Arthur.

"Perhaps you'll walk here every night until you remember the truth of what you saw," Joslin answered.

"That will never be," said Arthur.

"I can help you," said Joslin.

"You can't."

"I can try. You've got no one else. Listen to me. Think. Think back. Think hard."

"What about?"

"The night of the murder. A night like this. You were here. You must have been."

"*No!*" Arthur cried. "If I was here then I killed the poor nun."

"That's not so," said Joslin. "Not you, Arthur. *Think.*"

Arthur remained kneeling, mouth still working, though silently again. Joslin waited.

Arthur moaned. "This is too much." He put his hands each side of his ears as if he was trying to hold his brain in place. "My head is bursting." He dropped further to the floor and curled up in a ball, still with his hands round his head. His breath came in loud, short gasps as if he was in a fit. Joslin waited, fearful now about what he might have done to the poor priest.

Then Arthur slowly stood up. "I must hide," he

murmured. His voice sounded as if he was back in his trance. He moved behind one of the great pillars and stood with one hand on the scaffolding as if to support himself. Joslin stood up as well and went with him.

"See where the wooden baulks rise up and hold the pillars in place," Arthur whispered. Joslin didn't know whether he was talking to himself or to him. Had he gone back into his sleep? "See the shuttering at the top while the mortar dries. What a glorious work this is. See how only God's providence and the skill of His servants has stopped this mighty cathedral from crashing to the ground in ruin."

He was silent again and Joslin waited to see if he would continue.

"What devil has the gall to defile this work?" Arthur said at last. He must be in his trance again. "Some beast, something slimy, has crawled in here and made it all as nothing.'

Another pause. Then: "Listen."

Joslin listened. He heard nothing.

"A latch clicked. A door is opening. It's the west door."

Joslin knew it hadn't. He had carefully made sure it stayed open.

There was more silence. All Joslin could hear were Arthur's snatched breathing and the fast thudding of his own heart.

Then Arthur spoke again. Now his voice was higher, more urgent. He gripped Joslin's arm with furious strength. "It's here. The beast has come into the house of God. What shall we do to destroy it for ever?"

His eyes were fixed in a direction towards the west

door, down the body of the nave. He seemed to be seeing something very real. His grip on Joslin's arm tightened more. "What shall we do? *What shall we do?*"

"We wait," said Joslin quietly. "Tell me what you see."

Arthur answered. "I see a creature from hell. Is it a dragon or a serpent? It drags its long length up our cathedral just as the serpent dragged itself to Eve spitting its poison to the confusion of us all. It brings evil and death with it. Its head is like a man's. But it has a man's head for its tail as well. What abomination is this?"

Arthur was seeing *something*, that was certain. What could it be?

Then a sort of inspiration struck him. Had he seen the same monster that very evening? He must ask the sleeping man the question, whatever the consequences should he be suddenly torn out of his trance.

"Arthur, look again. Can you see its long body?"

"Oh, yes. There are great holes and gashes in it, as though it cannot sustain its own frame except by the power given to it by Satan."

Now came the question which could ruin everything. But he could think of nothing else to ask. "Arthur, is it a ladder? Are its head and tail really men at each end carrying it?"

There was a long silence. *I've lost him*, Joslin thought. *I've broken the spell and now we'll never know.*

But all at once, everything changed. Yes, the spell was broken but it was relief, not terror, which succeeded it. Arthur spoke normally, in a light, laughing voice. "Of course it's a ladder carried by men. What else could it be?"

"Are you awake?" Joslin asked.

"I think so. Unless you're in my dream."

"No," said Joslin. "I'm really here."

Not that there was much point, it seemed to him. Now the trance was over, the whole experience would vanish back into whatever place it came from, to torture Arthur with feelings of guilt.

"Do you want me to tell you what happened next?" Arthur said.

Joslin's heart leapt. He didn't expect this. "Can you?"

"Of course. I remember now. I see it happening again." He paused as if collecting his thoughts. "I'm not in a trance now, Joslin," he said. "But I can see it happening in front of me. It's a long ladder. There's someone at each end. They bring it up to just in front of us and put it on the ground. The first is saying, 'Help me lean it up against the scaffolding as the masons do.' The second is answering. 'Yes, master.'"

Silence again. Then: "There's moonlight through a transept window. It shines on the second man's face. I'm sure I know that face. It's small, shrivelled, hang-dog. They're swinging the ladder up to meet the scaffolding at its highest point. The first man is speaking. 'Go back to the lodge. Do nothing and say nothing. I'll come for you when we need to bring the ladder back. And then I'll see you one evening soon with a reward. Say one word and that reward's a dagger in your guts.' 'I understand, master,' says the second. I know that face. Who is he?

"The second man's going. I see the first man's face in the moonlight." He shuddered. "Oh, that's a face and a half, that is. I'd never forget *that* face. Look at those huge eyes, the hooked nose, full mouth. But I've never seen it before."

Joslin wondered whether, as soon as he described it to Crispin, he would say, "That's Luke, of course."

"I have to stay here," said Arthur. "I'm frightened. If he sees me I don't like to think what he'd do. But he's not going to see me. He's walking off, back down the nave. Has he gone? Surely he'll be back. He must have put that ladder up for something."

Arthur said nothing for a long time. Joslin found the silence unnerving. "What's happening?" he said.

No answer again. Time seemed to stand still: Joslin wondered if Arthur had lapsed back into sleep.

At last, Arthur said, "There's someone there." Another silence. "No, it's two people. They're coming up the nave together. One is tall. Is it the first man again? I don't. . ." He broke off and stared for a moment. Then he said, "The other one's a woman. She's standing close to me. I hear her breathing. I feel her trembling. She – she's in *ecstasy*, Joslin. She's feeling what saints feel and mystics know. She's feeling something denied to ordinary people like us. She's near to Christ, Joslin. She's been taken over by a great joy.

"The first one is talking in a whisper. I can hear the words. 'The angel. You want to see the angel. Let me take you to see the angel.' She's answering. Her words trip over themselves in her delight. 'Yes. Do. I must see him.' The first says. 'You go ahead. I'll watch over you. You'll not fall.'" Arthur's voice rose in an anguished cry. "Don't listen. Those are devil's words." His voice dropped. "It's no good. That's what I want to say. But the words won't come out. They're walking

139

up the ladder. She's first. The other is following. I'm watching a little creature with no defence stalked by a beast of prey."

He gripped Joslin's arm and turned his face to him. Tears were coursing down it. "She's gone, Joslin. I couldn't stop her. She won't come down again. If she'd heard me she wouldn't have gone. I sent her up there, Joslin. I've killed her."

"Arthur, you haven't. This would have happened anyway. You couldn't stop it – but now you'll bring the killer to his damnation."

Arthur said nothing. But when he next spoke his voice was calmer. "The other's coming down. Yes, alone. It's done. Now the murderer's walking away. The nave is empty." Another pause. Then: "Something's happening. The two men are here again. I see both their faces now. What's the first man saying? 'Never a word. You'll know what I'll do.' 'Yes, master,' says the other. I *do* know that second man. But I can't place him. They're taking the ladder down. They're a slithering monster again. They've gone."

Arthur let out a long sigh. "That's it," he says. "That's what I saw. It came back to me."

"It's why you felt guilty," said Joslin. "You can forget that now."

"I may. One day," Arthur replied. "Not yet." He shivered. "I'm very, very cold," he said.

"Get back to your bed," said Joslin. "You'll sleep properly now."

Joslin was back at the inn. He dreaded telling Crispin about the face Arthur saw. But he had to. "Huge eyes, hooked nose, full mouth. Does that mean anything to you?"

"Why should it?" Crispin answered.

"Tell me if it does and I'll tell you why. It isn't Luke's face, is it?"

"Nothing like him."

"Thank God for that. Now listen." He told him his experiences in St Ethelbert's with Arthur.

"I believe you," said Crispin. "Why shouldn't I? We may not know who he was but that doesn't mean others won't."

"We should tell Edwin," said Joslin. "We'll go first thing."

"We have other matters, more important," Crispin replied. "We need to go back to Luke's. Arthur can tell Edwin."

This morning, St Katherine's was quiet and busy, as if the nuns regarded Agatha's disappearance as part of

God's inscrutable will. Not for the first time in his life, Edwin wondered why people accepted fate so easily. Had he thought we were powerless to prevent evil, he might never have become a coroner or a Justice of the Peace, dispensing law and punishment.

He also wondered if he had made a mistake. Perhaps Freya didn't know as much about St Katherine's as Agatha did. She resolutely parried all his requests to say more about Christina with, "We never ask our novices about themselves. We must accept them for what they are. Only their priests and God will know their secrets."

He was getting nowhere. So he came clean. "What if I told you that I believe Christina arrived un-announced, in great distress. She came from very close by. She was Luke Thurn's sister and she had just had an experience so terrible that her hair turned white overnight."

Freya said nothing. Edwin looked at her. Was she weighing up a judicious answer or being deliberately stupid? Then, just before he said it all again, im-patiently this time, she spoke. "Of course you are right. Agatha knew and I did too. We felt we should defend her memory."

Edwin bit back a sudden huge anger. "You should have told me," he said. "The best way to defend Christina's memory is to find out who killed her. But Agatha has taken the law into her own hands and has made things far more difficult for me." He was getting angry. "Agatha should have told me what she was going to do. If she didn't tell you, it's the first thing you should have thought of." He stopped, calmed himself down, drew breath and spoke less heatedly. "That's a silly thing for me to say. Even if she didn't tell you, you might have guessed it. Your first duty was to tell me."

Now Freya spoke with a quiet intensity which made Edwin ashamed. "How dare you think my first duty is to you, or to any man? God will provide, not you. If it is His will, we wait for it as He thinks fit."

Edwin was humbled. "I'm sorry, manciple."

But Freya wasn't stopping. "Yet God has done stranger things than send unlikely vessels for carrying out His purposes. If he has chosen you as his agent we may marvel, but we must accept it. You are right. Agatha did know some of Christina's story, though not all, and I knew less. We recognized Christina because, alone in St Katherine's, we have business in the world outside. The sisters do not: their vows keep them here. Agatha did go without telling me where. Why shouldn't she? We've known each other long enough to divine each other's thoughts. She knew I'd realize what she had done. She also knew that I would never tell you. Unless, of course, God told me otherwise."

"I understand," Edwin replied humbly.

"We know Christina came from our near neighbour's place and that she was his younger sister. When she arrived she gabbled things we didn't understand about her elder sister and brother-in-law. We asked her to slow down and take her time, but she stayed incoherent. It was something about stones and something dark. 'Stones and darkness,' she cried and then fell in a dead faint. When she came round she wouldn't talk about it again. We never asked her to: if she wanted to tell us in her own time, she would. But she never did."

"Can you remember the exact words she used about her sister Madge and brother-in-law Gwylim?"

"I fear I can't. Nothing made sense."

"I see. What about this business of her hair?"

"Yes, that was strange. When she came here, in the dead of night, her hair was beautiful – but pure white. When morning came she said that she would stay and make her life with us, so obviously this hair had to be shorn off. We have no mirrors here to encourage vanity and we had tied Christina's hair back so she wouldn't see it. When she saw those lovely locks falling to the ground, she screamed. We weren't surprised: that's the sight which really tells new entrants what they've taken on. But this was more. She was hysterical. When we calmed her down, she cried, 'But my hair is black. Everyone knows my hair.' We thought as you did. Fear had turned it. We have heard of such things. She would tell us about that fear, we thought, when she was ready."

"But she never was," said Edwin.

"No," said Freya. "She never would while the fear gripped her and in time she forgot about her hair." The anger of both had died. They were thinking the same thing. They were talking about a girl who had seen devils. Edwin felt a strange comradeship in the room. When he spoke it seemed irrelevant. "Did she ever mention a golden angel?"

"Not to Agatha or me. Yes, I know all about Jude Cox and what he said to her. Mildred and Rosette told me. But I can't account for it."

"I must speak to Mildred and Rosette again."

"I'll have them brought here."

"But first I'd like to see Joan."

"Of course you may. You know your way to the stables."

So Edwin went, on his own, feeling that the last few

minutes might have made him accepted in the nunnery.

Joan was grooming the coat of Agatha's little pony as if making him gleam would magically bring his mistress back. She looked up with hope in her eyes. "Have you found her?" she asked in a small voice.

"I'm sorry, Joan. I've come to ask if you can help me."

"Anything."

"When Agatha's pony—"

"Daw," said Joan.

"When Daw came back was there anything on him which might have shown where he'd been? Any mud on his hooves and legs? Dust on his coat? Anything at all which shouldn't have been there?"

"Nothing!" Joan cried wildly. "Nothing at all. I've lain awake all night trying to think of something. But there was nothing."

He thanked her and left. When he came into the manciple's room, Freya was there with Mildred and Rosette.

"Thank you for seeing me again," he said. "Now, you remember the last time we spoke, about the mason Jude Cox, and what he said to Christina about a golden angel. I need to know something else, and I want you to think back carefully, because if you say something you aren't sure of, then finding Christina's killer and Agatha's whereabouts may both become more difficult."

"As if we would," said Mildred.

No, of course they wouldn't. He should remember his father: "There's more to these nuns than meets the eye."

"Right," he said. "Was there anything in what

Christina said or did that day or afterwards which showed that she knew about a golden angel, before Jude Cox mentioned it?"

They thought for some time. Then Mildred said, "Yes. She said, '*My* wonderful golden angel. How I long to see it *again*.' She must have known it already. I hadn't thought of that."

"You're sure about this?" Edwin asked.

"Yes," said Mildred. "Yes, I am. Definitely."

"So am I," said Rosette.

"But if you're right, then Christina knew Jude already," said Edwin.

"No, she didn't," said Mildred.

"But perhaps he knew her," said Rosette. "Or he knew about her."

"You heard what the coroner said, about being certain of what you tell him?" Freya reminded them. "How could a rough mason possibly know a sister mewed up in these cloisters?"

"But he must have done," said Rosette. "He knew who to talk to."

There was silence for a moment. Then Edwin said, "Thank you. You've given me much to think about."

Mildred and Rosette left. Edwin had another question. "Freya," he said. "How did you come to ask Jude Cox to repair your wall?"

"A stroke of providence," Freya answered. "Mildred reported the wall to me. She said that the mortar between the stone blocks had crumbled away and the blocks were loose. That very day, Jude Cox arrived to offer his services. He seemed plausible: he said he was a journeyman mason on his way from Hereford after working on St Ethelbert's, he was going home to Bromyard, and as he was passing he saw what a fine, substantial stone building St Katherine's was. It needed a wise pair of hands to keep it up to its proper state of repair. He asked if there was any job in the masonry line which needed doing. So I told him about the wall, reported by Mildred that very morning."

"I thought it was a manciple's job to inspect the nunnery regularly to see that all is in order."

"It is. I do. But I'm ashamed to say I had never noticed that wall."

Yes, now he was certain. "There'd be no need for shame if it didn't need repairing before that day," he said.

"What do you mean?"

"I mean that Jude Cox's turning up that morning was no coincidence. I believe he'd been watching the nunnery. I believe he knew Christina worked in the gardens with Mildred and Rosette. He broke into the grounds the night before to meddle with the wall, pull out the mortar and loosen the stones, to have the perfect chance to meet Christina and feed her nonsense about a golden angel where the city meets heaven. He knew it was exactly what she wanted to hear."

Freya took all this in without comment. Then she said, "If you're right, Christina was condemned from the moment she entered here and St Katherine's has been made sport of by evil men."

"I'm sorry," Edwin replied. "But that's how it seems to be. The question is, how did Jude Cox know Christina was here?" He thought for a moment. Then he said, "Sister Freya, is there no other nun who ever goes into the outside world?"

"One only," said Freya. "I'm sorry: I had forgotten

before. Sister Felicity. She has healing hands and a way with herbs and simples. It is not fair that she should cure only nuns: sometimes she goes outside to help the folk round about."

"I should like to see her," said Edwin.

Freya sent a novice to find her. A few minutes later, Sister Felicity arrived, old and wrinkled, but with a deeply wise look.

Edwin came straight to the point. "Sister Felicity, have you ever visited Luke Thurn's estates?"

"Twice that I can remember," she said. "Once years ago and once about six weeks past. Each time to cure tiny babies."

"And did you know Christina came from there?"

Sister Felicity looked suddenly ashamed. "Yes," she said. "I'm sorry, Sister Freya, but I couldn't help knowing her when she came here because I saw her at Luke Thurn's. I kept it to myself, though."

"I'm sure you did," said Edwin. "But, last time you were there, did you tell anyone that Christina was here?"

"Never," said Felicity. "I wouldn't—" Suddenly she drew in her breath sharply and clapped her hand over her mouth. "Oh. I'm sorry."

"Well?" said Edwin.

"It was when I had finished my work. A man escorted me out. He was rough and rude. I was angry. I remember now. I said, 'Christina would not like it if she thought the people she left here behaved so.' 'What do you mean?' he demanded. 'I mean nothing,' I answered and ran out across the road to my own place. Freya, what have I done?"

"Nothing," said Edwin. "You spoke well. You should not have to put up with rudeness." *Even so*, he thought, *now I know that someone at Luke Thurn's place knew where Christina was.*

He left soon after, with his mind racing. His short time in St Katherine's had been more useful than he had dared imagine. Would the visit to Luke Thurn's which he'd make right now help him as much?

Sister Joan stood outside the stables and watched him mount his horse and canter off. At that moment she had a vision, clear in every detail, of little Daw when he came trotting home alone, harness dangling. This time Joan saw clearly what had lain hidden at the back of her mind and eluded her through a sleepless night.

Yes, Daw did bring evidence with him. It was clear, it stared her in the face as she took his harness off, and she couldn't understand how she had come to forget it.

When Joslin woke that morning, he remembered Arthur's travail the night before, and felt as if they had come back from a far and dangerous journey together.

He pushed the thought away. Instead, he puzzled over something Edwin said last night that wouldn't go away: "Agatha, Mother Superior of St Katherine's, rode out of her nunnery. Her horse came back alone, but she has not been seen again." That was why Edwin went to St Katherine's. He had come away no wiser about Agatha, but with news of Jude Cox and golden angels.

"Why did Agatha go and where has she gone?" he said to Crispin as they ate a breakfast of bread and fish caught in the Wye.

"You tell me," Crispin replied.

"I believe she knew where Christina came from. You must have seen women like her. They think, no matter what scripture tells them, that it's men who are the weak creatures. She looked at Edwin and thought, *I don't trust you to find out who did this. I'll have to do it myself.*

"If Agatha knew where Christina came from and went to look for her killer, then she would go to Luke's house," said Crispin.

"And we were there yesterday," said Joslin. "Was she still there?"

"Not in the house itself," said Crispin. "We would have found her."

"What about the tower?" said Joslin.

"Yes, she could be. It would make a good prison. We must get inside it," said Crispin. "That's where we'll go this morning, back to the house. We'll talk to Hawkin again."

Joslin said nothing for a moment. He recalled something he had seen the day before – dark, narrow, suffocating, which made his stomach tight with fear.

"What about the well?" he said.

"What about it?" Crispin answered.

"Could she be in it? Think of being thrown down it, knowing that water has closed over your head and even if you could cling on and stay clear, there's no way back up for any mortal being."

Crispin considered this. Then he said, "I can think of it. Just as I think of Christina and her fear of being walled up."

Arthur woke. He sat up. A load had gone from his shoulders. He sprang out of bed. What was this new feeling that filled him?

Why, he was *happy*.

He remembered what happened last night. Joslin was right. His guilt was gone. A bright sun shone through his window. Birdsong sounded in the close outside. God's creation was beautiful again.

He dressed quickly. In the cathedral he robed to say

the day's first Mass. He was ready before Giles entered with Ivo de Trellick and the rest. "My lord, I will say Mass this morning. It is my duty," he said.

Even Ivo's face looked benevolent. Arthur tried a smile in his direction and – could it be true? Yes, it was. Ivo's mouth twitched, though whether through affliction or pleasure Arthur could not say.

What a wonderful day it would be. What a wonderful life he would have. Yes, he'd be a bishop one day. Nothing could stop him. And when Mass was over, he would go into the city to tell Edwin what had happened.

Mass went well. Giles praised him and Arthur answered, "The travail I was under has departed, by God's good grace." Giles nodded wisely and there, he hoped, was an end of the matter. As soon as he could he left the cathedral and hurried to Bridge Street. But by now, Edwin was gone.

The moment their horses had turned off the road into Luke's lands they knew something was wrong. There was still no sign of life, but a strange foreboding was in the air. "I don't like this," said Crispin.

"So you feel it too," Joslin answered. "Something bad has happened."

"Feel it? I can hear it," said Crispin. A low moaning came faintly from the cottages. "I hear anger."

"I hear grief," said Joslin.

Suddenly, there was a shout of "There they are!" Lud appeared from a cottage.

"I told you the murderers would return. Now we can see them."

Six men emerged. They were consumed with a rage

Joslin felt a hundred paces away. The minstrels reined in their horses and waited.

Lud led the men towards them. "They mean harm," Crispin muttered. "Get ready to go, fast." But fifty paces away, Lud stopped and motioned the others to stop too. "I knew you'd only come back to make trouble," he shouted. "You don't come sniffing round here after years away without leaving your mark. Luke always knew you were no good. But we never thought you'd come back to do murder."

"Murder?" cried Crispin. "I don't. . ."

Because of what happened next, Joslin wondered why Lud had stopped so far away to shout at them, like a soldier coming forward to parley with the enemy from a safe distance. But the others didn't seem to want to parley. There was no feeling now that Lud was ruling these people by terror. Everybody was united in anger

"You killed our neighbour," screamed one. "You killed our brother," shouted a second. "Hawkin's blood shrieks out," yelled another. Their faces were contorted with fury. They suddenly rushed past Lud towards Crispin.

"Out of here," Joslin shouted, turned Herry and spurred him on. He heard Cob's hoofbeats behind them. The horses galloped until they were far enough away on the road to be safe to stop and turn again.

The road in either direction was empty. "No matter how angry they get, these people never seem to leave their little acres," said Crispin. He spoke lightly, but Joslin could see he was breathing heavily.

"What did he mean, 'Hawkin's blood shrieks out'?" Joslin asked, though he knew perfectly well. His heart sank like lead. Death never stopped stalking him.

"Someone thought Hawkin told us too much." Crispin answered. His face crumpled. "Hawkin was a good friend. Is this what homecoming means, the deaths of my friends? I should have stayed in Arden Forest. At least I knew what the danger was there."

Joslin bowed his head. Poor Crispin. First Christina, now Hawkin. "We can't go back in there," he said. "We'd never get out again."

"I know we wouldn't," Crispin answered. "At least, not from the front for all to see. But I remember every inch of my own land. We'll be there."

Joslin followed Crispin off the road far out of sight of Lud and the peasants. "They'll never see us here," said Crispin.

They led the horses along an overgrown path lined by trees which hid them well. After a hundred paces, they stopped and tied their horses to a tree. Crispin looked at undergrowth running riot. "This place is in a terrible state," he said. "Why does nobody see to it?"

He moved on quickly, with Joslin keeping up. They came to the moat, here choked with dry reed and clinging tendrils, and pushed their way through. Then Crispin parted a mess of long grass, sapling suckers and overhanging branches and looked through a gap in the half collapsed wall.

"Do you see where we are?" he said. In front of them was the courtyard with the well in the middle. There was no sign of life.

"We can find our way into the tower in peace now," said Crispin.

Joslin felt apprehensive about this. "Lud's not stupid. He'll know we won't go away easily."

"Not him," Crispin replied. "Where he's stupid is thinking his threats can scare us off. I know him of old. But if Hawkin's dead, rest assured Lud killed him himself."

"Don't be too sure," said Joslin. "I think there's someone else around this place. I felt it yesterday and I still do."

"If we don't take risks, we'll get nowhere," said Crispin. "Now, follow me again."

They crept round the inner wall and the outbuildings, Soon they came to the window they had clambered through yesterday. It looked as though nobody had been near since. They scrambled through again, into the quiet, dust- and cobweb-encrusted solar.

"This place does seem smaller than I remember," said Crispin.

They moved out into the great hall, then to the door which led into the tower. The wooden barrier stared back impassively. They could only guess what bolts and locks secured it on the other side. Crispin said. "I'll take those swords and spears off the walls of the hall. We might crack a way through."

But Joslin was looking at the door thoughtfully. "This is a very strange tower if you can get out of it into the house but you can't get in," he said. "What's the point of building it?"

"What are you trying to say?" said Crispin.

"Who wanted this tower built?" Joslin went on. "Luke, I should think. Why? For his own safety, surely, so he could get in when he wanted to. But that didn't mean he wanted anyone to share it with him. I've known people like that. For most of my life I lived in a castle. They're full of odd stairways, secret boltholes, ways through where you don't expect them. People always knew the time might come when they had to disappear in a hurry. Perhaps Luke built a way in and out of the tower meant only for him."

"How are we supposed to find it?" Crispin growled.

"What about the one place he called his own. His solar. That could be the first place to look."

Crispin looked at Joslin admiringly. "You always surprise me," he said. "You have ever since we met in the Forest of Arden."

They went back to the solar. Joslin looked round. "Nothing here," he said. He opened the door to Luke's bedchamber. Nothing again.

"What are we looking for?" said Crispin.

"The entrance to a tunnel? A stairway? We won't know until we find it."

"There's no door or entry except what we've come through," said Crispin.

"There must be," Joslin replied. It stuck in his mind that there was something he'd heard which would give him a clue. What could it be? It must be very recent to refer to this place.

"When we came in here yesterday – and today – Crispin, you said, 'This room is smaller than I remember.'"

"I know," Crispin replied. "I'm sure it is. But it's a long time since I've seen it and I was much younger then, and smaller. The eyes play tricks sometimes. It doesn't matter."

"I think it does," Joslin replied. "Why should you think it's smaller?" He went on looking round the walls. "Have you noticed," he said, "that to get from the solar to the bedchamber you have to go through what's nearly a passage?"

"It only seems like a passage because the wall is so thick," said Crispin.

"Thick? It's nearly three whole paces."

"The wall holds the house up, of course."

"But you don't have inside walls thicker than the outside walls."

"That's just the way it's built."

"Do you remember it being so very thick?"

Crispin thought. "No," he said at length. "But I was only ever in here when Luke wanted to give me a good thrashing."

The lintel of the bedchamber door on one side let straight into the bedchamber wall. On the other side, where the wall seemed more like a passageway, hung a tapestry. It showed nuns at prayer, beautifully stitched, its colours well preserved where the sun never reached to fade them.

"I don't remember that," said Crispin.

"Look," whispered Joslin. He pointed to a figure on the tapestry, picked out perfectly in gold thread. "An angel, hovering over the nuns." Its wings were spread out as if protecting them: somehow its shape suggested infinite love and care.

"The golden angel again," said Crispin.

"Did Christina make tapestries?" asked Joslin. "It looks like her sort of scene. Perhaps she was thinking of being a nun already."

"Yes. That's her handiwork. That quiet girl who had a bad word for no one hardly did anything else. When I take my full inheritance, that tapestry will be hung in the place of greatest honour." He looked at it silently for a few moments. Then he said, "This is a strange place for Christina to put such a beautiful tapestry, where no one could see it." He lifted it up. "Ah!" he breathed.

Underneath the tapestry was a wooden door, small, set in the middle of the wall, more like the door to a cupboard. Crispin opened the latch. They saw narrow stairs leading upwards, dark at the foot but with a little light creeping in at the top. Joslin stepped up and on to the steps. Crispin followed, latching and bolting the door behind him. "That will stop anyone following us," he said.

Joslin started the climb towards the light. Crispin followed. "Luke must have built these stairs up against the solar wall and the walls of the room above and then built a new wall across to hide them," he said. "He went to a lot of trouble over this and the people who did it must have been paid well to keep quiet. Or kept quiet some other way."

They climbed for twenty steps. Then the stairs stopped. They were in a passageway, so low they had to stoop. Above them, thick wooden beams morticed into the wall sloped upwards. To their side, huge beams stretched upwards from the floor. The floor underneath was wooden, hardly a plank's width so they had to squeeze through. The walls each side were made of wattle and daub.

"The hall roofbeams above, the house framework to our side," said Crispin. "This passage is built inside the wall like the stairway."

"Where's the daylight coming from?" said Joslin.

"This is a tiny gallery all the way along the hall, right in the corner of the eaves," said Crispin. "You could only see it from the floor if you really looked for it. As it's built into the wall, it's almost invisible. The light comes in from the hall. He's left gaps between the roofbeams so he could see what went on in the hall without being seen himself."

Joslin looked. All the way along was a gap which let in light and air and also gave an uninterrupted view. "It's like a minstrels' gallery for dwarfs," he said.

They carried on the length of the hall and kitchens to the end. Crispin stopped. In front of them was a blank stone wall.

"We've come to the tower," said Joslin. "It's a dead end."

"It can't be," said Crispin. "There must be *some-thing*."

They pulled at the stone blocks in front of them, but they were well mortared in. They stepped back, sweating and defeated.

Crispin looked round. They were standing now on stone. For the last two feet of the passage, the walls either side were also stone. Above were flag-stones.

"The passage ends inside the tower wall, just as if it's been built inside the house wall," he said. "We'll try to move the flagstones over our heads."

They pushed, heaved and grunted with effort and at last one moved. Light came through. They heaved more until the flagstone had been shoved through and lay on the floor. Crispin pulled himself through, then stood, rubbing the back of his neck.

"I'm on a stone floor. There are arrow slits in the walls," he said.

Joslin followed him into the tower. The floor was no more than ten paces across. Arrow slits were set in the walls all round, three facing out each side. Next to where they had stepped out was a stone stairway built against the wall with no guard rail. It stretched upwards to the floor above. The mortar cementing the stone blocks of the wall together still looked new.

Joslin shivered. Now they were surrounded on all sides by thick stone walls and roofs, the air struck chill.

They stood still and listened. Then Crispin quickly climbed the stairs. Joslin followed. They reached the next floor. It was the same, except that the stairs were on the opposite side.

"The tower's empty," said Crispin. "As empty as the house."

There was a slight quaver in his voice, as if he were not really quite convinced. Joslin had a feeling he'd so often had before and never yet been wrong about. They were not in here unnoticed.

He looked through an arrow slit, at a tiny segment of the view of the cottages. He saw peasants in a group. Lud was unmistakable even at this distance. They were talking urgently to someone. He looked hard to see who it was.

"Edwin's there," he said.

"Well, let him be," Crispin answered. "It's no concern of ours."

Joslin didn't argue, though he knew it was very much their concern. Crispin was climbing the next steps up, towards where daylight showed. Joslin followed. They were on the roof, crouching behind the battlements. Joslin looked down to the shouting peasants and the listening Edwin, like tiny figures stitched into Christina's tapestry. He wondered whether those were Lud's sharp tones shrilling above the rest. He knew what they were saying.

"Lud will be making sure Edwin knows about Hawkin," he said. "And you know who he'll blame. Us."

"Let him," Crispin answered. "If Edwin's fool

enough to believe that conniving wretch, then he's not worth the time of day."

"We can't afford Edwin as an enemy," Joslin replied.

"Don't worry about him," said Crispin and disappeared back down the steps. Joslin followed, past one floor, two, three, then a fourth.

"We've reached the ground," said Crispin.

"But the stairs haven't stopped," said Joslin.

It was dark on the bottom floor, with no arrow slits in the walls. The cold was sharper. There was a rank, earthy smell. Crispin felt in his tunic for tinder. A little light flared. In the opposite corner another stairway led down into deep darkness from which more damp cold seemed to pour out. They listened.

Nothing. But Joslin's shivering was not now simply because of cold. All those fears of darkness, of being closed in, trapped, had returned.

"We're not alone," he said. He couldn't keep panic out of his voice. "There's something down there. It's waiting for us."

"If I want to finish what I came back here to do, then I have to meet it," Crispin answered. "Are you with me or not?"

Joslin took a deep breath and swallowed his panic. "Of course I am," he said.

Edwin knew something was wrong as soon as he turned off the road. This time the house did not stare back from an empty landscape. Men, anger wrapping them like a scarf, leaned on hoes and spades like soldiers waiting for battle with weapons at the ready. Edwin even had a fleeting fear the spades might be used on him. A thin man with a face he distrusted on sight stepped forward. "You are Edwin Pendock, Justice of the Peace," he said. It was a statement, not a question.

"I am," Edwin answered.

"Then we can solve all your problems at once. You have two murders already to deal with. Now you have a third."

"Who?" asked Edwin.

"Our friend and kinsman Hawkin. Done to death by villains. And we know who they were."

"Go on," said Edwin guardedly.

"Crispin Thurn, who hates his family, wants revenge for what happened years ago and would do anything to get it. And his miserable little friend who comes from the land of the king's sworn enemies and who would kill for a groat, like all his kind."

"You think so?" Edwin replied.

"We know so," the thin man shouted.

A few shouted agreement. But Edwin looked beyond. Some were silent. Not everyone agreed with the thin man. He caught the eye of an old man at the back. The old man gravely shook his head.

"Why are you so sure?" said Edwin.

"It's clear. These two come, as if they've just arrived after years away, they ask their questions and go. Then we find Hawkin dead."

"Why should you doubt that they just arrived? Crispin only came back to Hereford the day before yesterday after many years away."

"That's what they want you to think. I believe Crispin skulked secretly round the city for many months, seeing how the land lies, and brought his miserable little friend with him."

163

"How do you know those two murdered this Hawkin?"

"Because Hawkin foolishly went away with them as if there was more to tell than we had already said. After that we found him."

"Where?" said Edwin.

"We'll show you." The thin man led the way. Edwin was surrounded by tenants as if a prisoner. He noticed that the old man who shook his head was not among them. They took him back the way he came, across the road to the grove of trees where the second body had been found. "Throat slit from ear to ear," said the thin man. "It's obvious. Hawkin goes with them, out of our sight. Hawkin doesn't come back. We go looking and find Hawkin." He looked keenly at Edwin. "Quite a killing ground, this grove, isn't it," he said.

Edwin thought about this. One man was killed here. The other man wasn't, but was brought here when dead. It wasn't only a killing ground, it was a sinister mortuary as well.

"I can't take this on trust," he said. "I have to see the body."

"Nothing easier," said the thin man. "Come with us."

He led Edwin back to the cottages. In one, the blond-haired Hawkin was laid out on a rough table, blood cleaned from a wide slash across his throat. A young woman knelt beside him, softly sobbing.

Edwin examined the body. Nothing but the throat wound. He stiffly bent to the woman. "I'm sorry," he muttered. "I will do my best to find who killed him." The sobbing continued without pause.

Edwin straightened up. "Has a priest seen him?"

"There's been no priest here for many a year," the thin man said.

In exasperation, Edwin said something that had been on the tip of his tongue for a long time. "Why do you do all the talking for these people? Haven't they tongues in their heads?"

"They are too shocked to speak," the thin man replied, with a confidence Edwin found repulsive. "I know the world. These are simple folk so they leave it all to me."

Something is wrong with what I'm seeing and hearing, Edwin thought. "I shall send the priest from St Peter's," he said. "He will arrange for Hawkin's due ceremonies and proper burial."

"But you'll bring those two to justice," the thin man demanded.

"When I find them and question them, the law will take its course," Edwin replied.

He mounted his grey horse and it cantered away towards the road. He was trying to make sense of this encounter when a figure emerged from the bushes by the entrance. It was the old man. "Edwin Pendock," he called. "Listen to me."

Edwin stopped his horse and bent down to the white-haired, withered fellow. "I'm listening," he said.

"Never believe Lud. He's paid to lead intruders astray."

"Who by?" asked Edwin.

"Ah, if I were sure of that I could tell you everything about this business and free us all from our bondage."

"What bondage?"

"I'll say no more. If I do, I'll go the way of poor Hawkin. I may be old, but I'm not sure I'm ready for

165

that yet. Crispin and his friend never killed Hawkin. If you want to find them, look in Luke Thurn's house, for that's where they've gone, thinking they'll come out triumphant. But I fear different for them."

"What do you mean?" Edwin demanded.

"Don't ask me any more. I've said enough already to make it doubtful that I'll live till sundown. Just remember that old Coll it was who put you on the right path."

"Why do you fear for them, Coll?"

"Because I reckon that what lurks in that house wants nothing which enters ever to come out again. To go in is to sign your own death warrant."

"One thing more," Edwin said. "Do you know Jude Cox?"

"Too well," Coll answered. But before Edwin had a chance to ask what he meant, Coll had disappeared back into the undergrowth and Edwin was talking to the empty air.

The stairway was rough and steep. They had to feel their way down. Though his little tinder flare went out, Crispin led, counting the steps. "Nine," he said. "I'm standing on an earthen floor." Joslin followed. "Where are you?" he whispered when he felt beaten earth under his feet. "Here," Crispin replied. His voice sounded from the left. Joslin's terror of darkness, of being closed in, was greater than ever. He moved towards the voice – and suddenly sprawled over stone blocks. "What's happened?" he gasped.

Another flare of tinder. Now he saw Crispin. He was indeed standing on an earthen floor. But it was littered with rough blocks of stone, as if a demented creature had pulled the foundations away.

"I see no point in staying down here," said Crispin. "If someone doesn't want us, I'd rather face him where I can see what I'm doing and move without breaking my neck on boulders."

Joslin picked himself up. He was trembling. "Let's go back where it's lighter," he pleaded.

They felt their way back up the steps. The dim light

167

of the bottom floor was broad daylight by comparison. Joslin's fright subsided.

"Is someone trying to make the tower collapse by tearing the foundations away?" said Crispin.

"And bring it all down on our heads?" said Joslin. "Surely not. Perhaps the stones are still being mortared in."

"You make your foundations first, not after the tower has been built," said Crispin.

Joslin sat on the floor and folded his arms round his knees. "These stones make me think of somebody looking for something." he said.

"Listen," said Crispin.

Joslin listened. Scrabbling and snatched, wheezy breathing. "Quiet," he whispered. "It comes from down below."

When Coll left him, all Edwin could think of were his last words. "*What lurks in that house wants nothing which enters ever to come out again. To go in is to sign your own death warrant.*"

What could that mean? He remembered the first time he saw the tower and had had an instinct that someone was inside, and a disturbing fancy that something lived at the bottom of the well. If Coll was right, that was the end of Crispin and the Frenchman. The body left in the trees had certainly been meant as a warning. What should he do?

He wasn't going in after them, that was sure. Not now, not alone. But sooner or later he knew he would. There was only one thing to do. He clicked his tongue, jerked the reins and the grey horse cantered back to Hereford and the next stage of Edwin's campaign.

They waited. The hair on the back of Joslin's head prickled with terror. Someone was coming up the steps. He closed his eyes. Then he heard Crispin say, "How did you. . .?"

Joslin opened his eyes and nearly laughed. There stood old Coll. "Thank God I found you in time," he said.

"What are you doing here?" said Crispin, surprised.

"I want you to come out before it's too late," the old man replied. "It doesn't matter what happens to me, but I want you safe. I know more than the others. I'm an old man: nobody cares what I do. So I can watch and listen and think and nobody interferes with me. I piece things together from scraps that some want kept secret and I know enough to make me very afraid for you. I fear Lud, and I fear those behind him even more. So should you."

"But there's nobody besides us in house or tower," said Crispin.

"Don't you believe it," Coll replied. "You're never alone here. There's more ways in here than you know of. Now, follow me."

"We know there's another way, through Luke's solar," said Joslin. "We found it and used it "

"I never knew about that one," said Coll, surprised.

"Well, you're going to know about it now," said Crispin. They led him up the steps to the floor above. Crispin found the groove at the side of the flagstone, pulled it up and squeezed himself into the opening. Joslin pushed Coll through after him.

"What are you doing to me?" Coll cried in alarm.

"Letting you get into the passage," Crispin answered.

"This place is full of passages," said Coll. "I found two myself that weren't here in your father's day."

"How many passages are there, then?" said Crispin.

"Two that I know of," Coll answered. "Three now you've told me about this one of Luke's. I know of two tunnels dug into the cellar down below us. They go out and under the ditch. One leads to Simon's old house, the bailiff's cottage, the other out to the road."

"Did Luke dig those as well?" said Crispin.

"I don't know."

"What are all these passages for?" Crispin asked.

"Strange things happen here," Coll replied. "Things which I don't understand yet but which keep me awake at night."

They filed along the passage over the hall, down the steps and back into Luke's solar. "Are we safe here?" asked Crispin.

Coll didn't answer. He was looking at Christina's tapestry with its golden angel, and was frantically making the sign of the cross, not like one seeing a holy object, but as if warding off some appalling evil.

Joan hardly dared touch this sign of where little Daw had come from. Freya must see it first. If Joan told people she had made wonderful discoveries, no one would believe her because she was old and of little account. Besides, she needed Freya to interpret the sign for her. She hobbled as fast as her ancient legs would take her to the manciple's room. Freya was poring over ledgers, but looked up willingly when she saw the old nun and left her work at once when she knew the reason.

In the stable, Joan took Daw's saddle from the wall.

"Look at that," she said. "Agatha is telling us where she is."

Freya looked at the saddle and Joan's trembling hand pointing to marks on it. Freya made little of them in the stable's half-light. "I need the sun to understand this," she said.

Outside, she peered again at the saddle. "Words are scratched on the leather," she said. "I can't read them." Freya wrinkled her forehead. At last she spoke. "It says, 'Thurn'. Then 'trees'. Then something else."

"Yes?" said Joan breathlessly

"Does it say 'way'?" said Freya. "And what comes after? It's a meaningless shape. It could be 'in' or 'up'. Agatha didn't have time to finish it. 'Thurn. Trees. Way' – way what? I can't tell."

"What's happened to Agatha?" Joan wailed.

"She went to Thurn's place, but had no time to tell what she saw."

"What are we to do?"

"I'm sorry, Joan. I have to leave. I must see Edwin again."

Edwin overtook Freya half a mile from the city gates. Her bony nag seemed on its last legs. He slowed his own horse to a walk and they rode together into the city.

"I have news," said Freya. "A discovery made after you had gone today, though it may mean nothing."

"Any news is welcome," said Edwin. "But let it wait until we're at my house, in quiet and comfort."

Once inside, Edwin led Freya to his upstairs solar and motioned her to sit at his table while he paced the room expectantly. Freya had brought the saddle with her. She placed it on the table and told Edwin what Joan found. Edwin looked at the scratches. "'Thurn? Trees?' Is that what it says? Then something I can't make out," he said.

"I thought it could be 'way', 'in' or 'up'," said Freya

"You're right," said Edwin. "It could. It could also be 'to'. Agatha undoubtedly went to Thurn's place. She could be writing 'tower'. Then she was interrupted and Daw ran off."

"What can have surprised her so?" asked Freya.

172

"That, Freya, is something I have no more idea about than you do. Pray God it was not something terrible." They looked at each other, mystified. "I've been to that house and the grounds around it twice since Agatha disappeared," Edwin continued. "I've spoken to tenants and have seen the body of a man viciously done to death there. I do not like the place. But nothing of Agatha have I seen nor heard."

"Shall you go again?" asked Freya timidly.

"If I must, I must," Edwin replied. "But after this morning, that place will be almost barred to me. I don't think I'd find anything on a third visit because few there will dare talk."

He said no more. The discovery had got him nowhere. He felt useless in front of this woman of God who assumed her earthly worries were safe in his hands. For almost the first time in his life, he wished he did not have the job he had taken on so many years before. He had reached the end. What more could he do? He said as much to Freya.

"That can't be true," she answered. "God will show you a way."

He'd better hurry up then, Edwin thought but, because of the company he was in, did not say.

He looked hopelessly out of his solar window, down at Bridge Street. He scanned the scene outside almost sightlessly. But then he snapped back into attention. Someone familiar strode towards the house. Arthur Rawle. But a different Arthur Rawle from the nervous, shifty wretch of the last two days. He walked with a spring in his step. His face was split with a broad smile of sheer happiness.

There was a hammering on the front door. A moment later, Arthur was shown up, flushed and

173

elated. "Edwin, you're back," he cried. "I called before. I have so much to tell you." Then he saw Freya. He bowed slightly. "Sister," he said, "is there any news of Agatha?"

"No," Freya answered. "But your happiness shows God has wrought a great change in you. If He can do that, I know He will give Agatha back."

"Have you found out who killed Christina yet?" Arthur asked. Their faces told him the answer. "Then listen to what I shall tell you."

He told how he felt such panic at the nightmares he could not remember and the strange guilt that he felt after he found Christina's body. He said how he was convinced that a devil had entered his soul, especially when he found himself back in the cathedral – though he knew he slept. And then he told them of his blessed release, when Joslin had helped him back to seeing that terrible night again.

"Where is this getting us?" said Edwin.

"Patience," said Freya. "The boy has great revelations to make."

"With Joslin by my side, I was taken back to that night in the cathedral as surely as if it were still happening in front of me. I saw the murder of Christina take place. I saw two men set the ladder up. I saw someone lead a woman up the ladder. I heard them talk and I made out some of what they said. They spoke of an angel." Edwin heard Freya catch her breath suddenly. "I saw the murderer come back down alone and then the two men taking the ladder back out. For brief instances, I saw their faces in the moonlight."

"Who were they?" said Edwin.

"I did not know the first one. But I know I have seen that face before, and the more I think of it, it was somewhere round the cathedral. The other I did not know either, at least not at once. But now I know him, because I have just seen him."

"Who was he?" said Edwin, hardly daring to expect an answer.

"Ulf," Arthur replied.

Edwin was disappointed. A man of no account doing a job of no account, mere fetching and carrying, probably too stupid and frightened to say anything worth hearing – how far did that get him?

"Arthur, you said you saw both faces," said Freya. "What was the one like that you did not recognize?"

Arthur shuddered. "Even though I was dreaming, I will not forget it. He had large, staring eyes, a full, sensuous mouth and a hooked nose almost out of proportion to the rest of his face. It seemed to me an evil face and his voice was the voice of evil."

Edwin suddenly snorted. "This is ridiculous. I can't take the testimony of dreams."

"You don't have to," said Freya. "This is one of God's strange ways. Some of His people will rise in their sleep and walk abroad, seeing all manner of things which, when they come back to their beds and wake again, they have forgotten. I believe that sometimes, if a person walking in sleep has witnessed an act of terrible evil, God will call that knowledge from him in ways which we cannot understand. I do not believe Arthur was cursed with a devil. I believe he was blessed by God, and given God's all-seeing eye. And this Joslin knew it as well."

"Why should you say that?" Edwin asked.

"Because Arthur might not know the face he saw but, once he described it, I did. It was Jude Cox, the journeyman mason."

"That's why I thought I knew him," said Arthur. "I must have seen him working with Hubert's men when I first came here."

All four looked at each other. Edwin felt a definite sensation of scales falling from his eyes.

"Could this make Agatha's message any clearer?" asked Freya.

Edwin seized the saddle again. "Let's assume this says 'to' and it's a start at writing 'tower'," he said. "Which tower? The cathedral's or Thurn's? If it's the cathedral tower, perhaps she's saying that she has found some secret which proves Christina's murder was plotted from Thurn's place. If she means Thurn's tower, she might mean she has found that the second body was thrown from it. It's very likely the second body is this same Jude Cox. Robin and Abel are sure of it."

"What if it's not?" said Freya.

"I cannot bear to think there might be more dead bodies to find," Edwin replied. "I've seen three in three days now." Then he wished he could bite his tongue out. Freya was looking at him and he knew she was wondering if Agatha would yet be the fourth.

"How could Agatha have seen the body in the trees?" said Arthur.

"We don't know what she saw," Edwin replied. "Did she see him in the rowan trees before we did?

"Are you so sure 'to' means 'tower'?" asked Freya

"No," Edwin admitted. "What you thought is just as likely. 'In', 'out', 'up' – who can tell?"

"Agatha has left us riddles to solve," said the nun.

"But we know this," said Edwin. "Jude Cox murdered Christina and then in turn was murdered himself, very likely in the same way. Why?"

Arthur looked distressed. "No," he cried. "No, that's not right."

"What do you mean?" said Edwin, annoyed. "It must be. If it's not, then we're wasting our time."

"But didn't I say?" Arthur cried. "Whoever took Christina up the ladder was not the person who brought the ladder in with Ulf."

Edwin sat down heavily and covered his face with his hands. "So there's someone new to find," he groaned. "What devil's brew is this?"

"I think you have a lot to tell us, Coll," said Crispin. "What have you found out already?" Coll replied. "What did poor Hawkin tell you before they killed him?"

"That a month after Gwylim married Madge and took her back to Wales, Luke went to visit them. He took his steward with him and said nobody was to question his action or go after him however long he was away. Christina would look after the house and see to the land."

"That's right," said Coll. "What did he tell you next?"

"That after a month Luke came back without his steward. Soon after that he started building the tower. He told Hawkin that he was building it to guard himself against *me*, as if he feared I'd bring an army to claim my rights. I suppose I should be flattered."

"Don't be," said Coll. "I don't think it's a defence against you. I think he would have been overjoyed to see you back, seeing what happened next."

"What was that?" asked Joslin.

"I don't know everything and some of it I have to guess. It was then that Lud became a trial to us. Luke used him to rule the men working on the tower with a harsh rod."

"I'm not surprised," said Crispin. "I know him of old."

"Luke needed someone he could trust to keep such a crew of strangers in order. Luke gathered round him masons who gave up their trade to stay here, labourers, old soldiers." He paused, as if this memory was not good.

"Why?" said Joslin after it looked almost as if Coll were too saddened by these thoughts to continue.

"Crispin," said Coll, "you know that under your father this was a happy place. In fact it was a happy place until you left that first time."

"I know it wasn't happy when I came back to find my father dead and my sisters locked away like prisoners," Crispin growled. "Where is Luke? Is he here? You must know that."

"Crispin, I don't. He may be in the bailiff's house. Lud says he is, but if that's true he keeps completely to himself. I don't know why."

"What happened to my father?" asked Crispin. "I'll never believe his death was a natural one."

"I fear you're right," said Coll. "But I can't tell you. I don't know."

"If the tower isn't defence against Crispin, what is it for?" asked Joslin.

"I don't know that either," Coll replied. "But whatever it is, it means no good to any of us. And one thing I'm sure of: that cursed golden angel is at the root of it. Do you remember how the sisters were locked away when Luke drove you out?"

"I do. I should have stayed and fought for them. It's my sin that I did not."

"Well, be sure that as soon as Gwylim came courting, they were let out and queening it as though never a wrong word had been said. Oh, we saw a lot of them all then. Madge, beautiful and a catch for any man; Christina still a fresh-faced girl with that wondrous hair; Luke every inch the prosperous lord in his own lands. No wonder Gwylim couldn't rest until he made Madge his own. At last, the arrangements were complete, the dowry settled and Luke seemed satisfied. It was then that we heard the first talk of the golden angel. Gwylim said it was his greatest possession. When he heard this, Luke became angry and said the settlement had to be changed. He thought Madge would be a greater possession for Gwylim than any golden angel and God gave no man such fortune as to have both. We heard no more about this argument after that, but soon Gwylim and Luke seemed well satisfied with what they had decided."

"You mean the angel was part of the settlement?" said Joslin. "Gwylim gave Luke the angel in exchange for Madge? Surely not."

"Surely not indeed. But I sometimes wonder if Luke thought he should. When I think that, then my feeling that it's a curse is strongest."

"Carry on with what happened," said Crispin.

"The marriage, when it came, was a grand affair. It took place in the chapel of the Blackfriars and afterwards there was feasting here for a week. Oh, we all had splitting heads then, I can tell you. Gwylim had brought the angel with him. It stood high in the banqueting hall and even we poor peasants sitting below the salt could see it shining as if it was God's own messenger sent to bless the wedding. Perhaps that was why Welsh and English didn't start fighting and why no greater joy and happiness had been known here since the days of your father, Crispin."

"It soon changed, it seems," said Crispin sourly.

"It changed the moment Luke went to Gwylim's accompanied and came back alone. Nothing good has happened here since. He built the tower as if the Welsh had the Scots and French for allies and were attacking tomorrow. He surrounded himself with workmen who seemed more like a garrison to keep everyone out, including us. Lud began to act like a jailer and Luke's workmen like a conquering army. But they suffered as well. Once we found one of them dead – stabbed. Was it a fight among themselves? Or did Luke do it? Life has been a living nightmare ever since."

"Hawkin said Luke took another journey afterwards," said Joslin.

"He did. After the tower was finished. We never knew he was going until there was a great to-do one night in the house. That must have been a leave-taking indeed, with all the lights and noise, shouts and screams. None of us dared to go and see what was happening. Next morning when light came, all seemed peaceful and quiet. But it was not a good quiet. I felt something strange and fearful about that quiet and I wasn't the only one. None of us bondmen have seen Luke or Christina since."

"So Luke never came back from this new journey," said Joslin.

"Yes, he did." Now Coll was silent for a moment,

as if he was wrestling with things beyond his understanding. "Lud is Luke's voice here now and Lud says he did. Lud says he's here, but the big house is abandoned and he'll never show himself again until his time is right."

"Great God above, what does that mean?" cried Crispin in exasperation. "Is this the right time, now I'm back to challenge him?"

"Nobody knows. All I know is that none of us have seen him."

"Then how can you believe Lud?" said Joslin.

"Because we know *somebody* is here. We often see lights in the tower: someone moves from floor to floor at night."

"Who?" cried Crispin. "There's nobody in the tower or house. We've been everywhere in them."

"What did you mean by saying Luke's workmen were like a conquering army?" Joslin asked.

"Some of those who built the tower stayed to be a bodyguard for him," Coll replied. "They're the ones who make this place a living hell. They have cottages round the old bailiff's house where we suppose Luke is. That part of the estate is closed off to us: none of us dare go near. They watch us, they stop us leaving, they treat us worse than any serfs on the cruellest baron's estates. There's an army circling house and tower, to defend it against us and anybody else."

"Nonsense," said Crispin. "Twice we've come here. Nobody stopped us, nobody even saw us. The place is deserted."

"So you think," said Coll. "I tell you you're watched. None of us can move without it being known. But I'm too old to care any more."

"Why are we allowed to go unchallenged?" asked Crispin.

"They know who you are," said Coll. "I reckon that somehow or other they knew you were on your way. They want to know whether you'll be more use alive or dead, before they decide it's time for you to see them."

"Then why don't we go straight to the bailiff's house and demand to see Luke?" said Crispin. "I have every right to. I lived in that house for half my boyhood."

"You'd not take a step near it and stay alive," Coll answered.

Joslin had another question. "You said you've seen neither Luke nor Christina since that night. Does that mean you think Christina went on this journey with Luke?"

"We thought she must have. Nobody was left in charge of the house this time."

"And did she return with him?"

"If Luke did, then so she must have. I haven't seen her either."

Crispin spoke. "Hadn't you heard that a nun from St Katherine's was thrown to death from the cathedral tower two nights ago? Her name was Christina. She had a passion for golden angels which may have led her to her doom. Her hair, though, was pure white, not black."

Coll did not answer yes or no. Instead, he said, "Two nights ago there was more shouting from the tower. We tried to see as much as we could in the moonlight without being seen. Some of us with sharper eyes swear a man was thrown from the top of the tower. But next morning there was nothing to show if we were right or wrong."

"Two people thrown to death in the same night. The body of the second was left in the rowan trees by the road for any traveller to see," Joslin mused. Then he said, "Edwin Pendock wonders if the dead man was a mason named Jude Cox. Do you know that name?"

Coll said nothing. The name had given him a shock. At length he murmured, "Jude Cox. One of Luke's trusted men and now one of Lud's. Why should they kill one of their own?"

"Trusted?" Crispin scoffed. "Not very much, it seems."

"But he was," Coll answered. "He oversaw the work on the tower. He found the workers and arranged for stone to be brought in. Luke thought a lot of him. We haven't seen him for three whole months."

"We've heard he worked on the cathedral tower until the master mason sacked him and then he turned up at St Katherine's to do some work, found Christina and fed her all sorts of rubbish about a golden angel on top of St Ethelbert's," Crispin said.

Coll wrinkled his brow in puzzlement. "We knew nothing of that," he said. "You see? The golden angel again. Those words fill me with terror because I know they're at the heart of everything."

"Yes, but how?" cried Crispin.

Coll did not answer.

"If nobody knows, we must work it out for ourselves," said Joslin.

"I must leave you," said Coll. "I'll have been missed by now."

"Go out of the window," said Crispin. "It's how we got in."

They helped him scramble through and saw him

disappear round the side of the house. "Back to his servitude," said Crispin. "Poor Coll."

Edwin, Freya and Arthur were in the mason's lodge at the cathedral. Hubert faced them.

"Arthur, describe the man you saw," said Edwin.

"He had big, deep eyes, full lips and hooked nose," said Arthur.

"Does that remind you of anyone, Hubert?" asked Edwin.

"That ne'er-do-well Jude Cox of course," Hubert replied. "Where did you see him?"

"In the cathedral the night Christina was murdered," said Arthur.

"Then why did you keep quiet about it?" said Hubert impatiently. "Afraid of what the bishop might say?"

"The reason is one sanctioned by God," Freya intoned impressively. Hubert looked at her, opened his mouth to say something, thought better of it and kept quiet.

"I saw Ulf as well," Arthur added quietly.

Hubert turned red with anger. "That nincompoop," he shouted. "Edwin, before I turn him over to your justice, I'll flay him alive myself."

"None of God's creatures, however unworthy, deserves that," Freya murmured.

Edwin agreed. "Quiet, Hubert," he said. "Let's hear what the poor fellow has to say for himself."

They did not have far to look. Ulf was crouching in the corner of the wall between cathedral and lodge. He had heard every word. He was shivering with fear. "Don't have me hanged, Master Edwin," he gabbled. "I didn't know what was happening, honest I didn't."

"You lied that morning and I believed you," Hubert roared.

"He made me." Ulf's voice was a scared squeak. "He said that if I didn't, I'd get a knife in my guts like my father did, but if I carried it through he'd come back at night and reward me well."

"And has he?" shouted Hubert.

"No, master," said Ulf.

"Serves you right," said Hubert.

"I'm sorry, Ulf," said Edwin. "You shouldn't have trusted him."

Ulf burst into tears and his thin shoulders shook. They could just make out what he said. "I'll be hanged and get nothing out of my folly."

"You should have thought of that before you. . ." Hubert roared. But Edwin interrupted him. "Don't worry, Ulf. I won't have you hanged." he said. "Now, it was Jude Cox, wasn't it?"

Ulf stopped crying and nodded.

"And what did you have to do for this money?"

"Make sure the store was open when he came, leave the ladder so we could take it out easy-like, put it back so no one would notice and lock up again so all was as before."

"But you didn't put it back quite right," Hubert growled. "*I* saw."

"Did he make you help carry it into the cathedral?" asked Edwin.

"He never said nothing about that until the night. 'I'll never manage this on my own,' he said when we'd got it outside. 'You'll have to help me.' I didn't want to because I was scared, but he said I'd get no money if I didn't. So I had to."

"And what did you think he wanted to do with the ladder?"

"He said he was supposed to do a job when he was

working here, but Hubert threw him out before he could finish it. He'd come back to make it the way it ought to be because that was the sort of man he was. He couldn't bear to leave things undone."

"But he never told you what it was?"

"He said I wasn't a mason so I wouldn't understand."

"You never saw Christina?"

"It was dark. When I came out, I saw someone waiting by the west door. I didn't know who it was, but somehow he made me afraid. Then I saw two people go in."

"Was Jude one of them?"

"I thought he must be. But I couldn't really say."

"Ulf," said Arthur, "I know Jude wasn't one of them. Did you see nothing which could help us tell who it was?"

"No, master. Except that only one came out and that was the one that made me feel feared."

"What did you think when only one came out?" asked Edwin.

"I didn't think anything."

"Did you hear a scream or something heavy hit the ground?"

"No, Master Edwin." Ulf thought again, then he said, "I might have heard a scream, but I thought it would be drunken folk in the city."

"What did you think when you knew a body had been found?"

"I was frightened."

"Why weren't you frightened when we spoke to you?"

"I wanted my money off Jude," said Ulf.

Hubert snorted with disgust. "You're not worth feeding," he said.

Arthur felt a sudden rush of compassion for the half-starved creature. So did Edwin: he put an arm round the thin shoulders and said, "Courage, Ulf. You'll not be hanged."

They left him crouched abjectly in the mason's lodge. Edwin's forehead was wrinkled with thought. What a mess it was. Yet everything pointed the same way. An unknown killer had been in St Ethelbert's, with a man now dead, who was connected with Luke Thurn's place. An old man there had said it was doubtful if he would live till sundown. Agatha was probably there as well, possibly dead already, but if not, then needing to be got out as soon as possible. The two minstrels had entered the place and the old man doubted if they would ever come out. There was nobody to bring good out of such a nest of evil as Luke Thurn's house except himself.

As far as he could see, there was only one possible course left for him to take, and it would need some quick and desperate organizing.

After Coll had gone they sat silent for some time. Then Joslin said, "We have to make some sense out of this."

"How?" Crispin grunted.

"Remember, Luke went to see Gwylim after the marriage," said Joslin. "He started out with his steward, but came back alone. Perhaps he had the angel with him then."

"What happened to the steward?" said Crispin. "If you're right, did Luke escape with the angel, but Gwylim kill the steward as he tried to get away with him?"

"Or would Luke kill his steward himself, because he was party to the theft and Luke didn't trust him?" said Joslin. "Or perhaps he was furious at what he saw Luke do – the worst act of a guest to his host, to steal his greatest possession. Or perhaps the steward stayed with Gwylim. Perhaps, after that, he felt his duty was with Madge, not Luke."

"This is all nonsense if Luke didn't steal the angel. But if he did, *where is it now*? Answer me that, Joslin."

Joslin said nothing for a moment. Then: "It must be here."

"What do you mean, here? I don't see it."

"It's hidden."

"Where?"

"I don't know," said Joslin. "But consider this. Coll said there's someone in the tower at nights. They see a light moving from floor to floor. We saw stones strewn over the ground in the lowest floor, as if someone has been tearing them out of the walls. All the stones in the walls above look newly mortared, as if they've been taken out lately and replaced."

"So?" said Crispin.

"Is the golden angel hidden inside the walls of the tower? That could be one reason Luke built it – it's not only a defence, it's a huge hiding place for a small thing. Someone is patiently looking for it."

"That's ridiculous," Crispin answered. "Coll said Luke is here, in the old bailiff's house, even though they never see him. Why should Luke have to search for something he hid himself?"

"Coll only thinks that because Lud told them so."

"This would all come clear if I could speak to Luke face to face," said Crispin. "Before this day's out, I mean to."

"The biggest question is, what really happened the night Luke and Christina were supposed to set out for Wales? Remember what Coll said? 'That must have been a leave-taking indeed, with all the lights and noise, shouts and screams.' Could it have been then that Christina went to the nunnery? Might that be the key to what's happened since?"

They seemed to have reached the end of the argument. Neither spoke for some time. And then Crispin said, "There's only one way to settle this. If you're right and all the floors above have been searched, then if the angel is here at all it must be in that cellar under the ground. Even in there, there can't be many possible places left. Although it's dark as pitch, we'll have to go back down and look for ourselves."

The more Edwin thought about Luke Thurn's house, tower and domains, the more a bed of sheerest evil, place of misery, seat of death they became. There were good people in there who must be brought out. Thinking about it would do no good: he had to take the law into his own hands. What commonsense could not do, brute force must.

He left Freya and marched back to Hubert. He needed to treat this carefully: Hubert was very prickly about having his work disturbed.

"Hubert," he said when he found him. "You'll agree we have a boil here which must be lanced now or we may all suffer. There's a cloud over this cathedral and over your work here."

"You're right," said Hubert. Then he looked at Edwin narrowly. "You're after something, aren't you? Come on, out with it."

"I want fifteen of your strongest, most fearless men."

"All my men are strong and fearless. Why do you want them?"

"They'll be part of an army to break down whatever plague has its seat in Luke Thurn's house, for I'm sure that's where it lies. I want Agatha rescued, an old man and two minstrels saved, a murderer found. I want your men armed with their picks and shovels and whatever other weapons they may have, which they haven't told you about, and I want them ready for anything, even death, if the battle goes against us."

"What good will my few men do on their own?" Hubert growled. "You want proper soldiers."

"I'll find them. I shall take whatever small garrison is still in the castle and empty the guardhouse of each city gate of watchmen. I'll have a force which will strike fear into most hearts round here."

"I won't order my men," said Hubert. "You'll have to ask them yourself. If this work's not finished because all my workmen are dead or wounded, then you'll have Ivo de Trellick to answer to. I won't bear the blame. And unless you get soldiers and watchmen as well then I really will give my men orders. I'll order them not to go."

"I'll take the chance," said Edwin. Ten minutes later he had eighteen volunteers and took the lot. Hubert looked at the empty scaffolding and decided he'd better go himself as well.

"We'll meet at Byster's Gate in an hour's time," said Edwin.

Just then, a small figure crept out of the masons' lodge. "Let me come too, Master Edwin," pleaded Ulf. "I'll not get in your way."

"*You?*" shouted Hubert. "Get back to your place, you little runt."

"Let him come, Hubert," said Edwin. "He needs to make amends."

As Crispin lifted Christina's angel tapestry and they climbed the narrow staircase, Joslin felt a strong foreboding of evil which stayed with him as they pushed their way along the cramped passage under the eaves. Crispin shifted the flagstone and was swinging himself up into the tower. Joslin followed and was about to replace it. But Crispin said, "No. Leave it open. You don't know if we'll have to get out in a hurry." So Crispin feared the worst as well.

Crispin had tinder ready and before they descended the last steps he lit it. As soon as they were on the earthen floor he held the light close to the wall and explored it carefully. "If someone works down here each night, then we'll find some means of light," he said.

After a moment he said "Ah. A candle-holder let into the wall. Nothing in it. But a holder might mean candles nearby." He continued looking. In one corner he found what he wanted. A box full of candles. He pulled one out, pressed it into the holder and lit it. There was a sputtering and then a smell: the candle was made of cheap mutton fat. But it gave a sort of light.

Now they could see the walls of the square cellar. In two corners were dark patches. They took candles to each and found they were holes big enough to crawl through. Cold draughts blew in from each one.

"Coll said there were two tunnels into this place," said Joslin. He shuddered, remembering his dreams and the tunnel into the castle at Stovenham. "I hope I never have to go along one."

The stones littering the ground came from one wall. The rest were in place. The light was too poor to show if they were still untouched or had been mortared back in. About a quarter of the wall being worked on was still intact. Crispin pulled at a block. He could not move it.

"This is no use," he groaned. "We need wedges, chisels, hammers."

"We'll have to go outside and look where all the old ploughs and harrows are," said Joslin.

"Not if we can help it," Crispin answered. "If there are candles here, there must be tools as well."

He lit another candle and searched the floor. A grunt of triumph showed he had found something. He picked up a hammer. Joslin took a candle, lit it off the candle in the holder and searched as well. They found, scattered on the ground and under stones, three chisels, two large wedges and another hammer. "Thrown all over the place," said Crispin. "Whoever searches here must get very impatient."

They stuck the candles in their own fat on stone blocks on the ground and started chipping at the wall in the flickering, uncertain light. Many stones were too large and set too deep even to attempt to move them. After two hours of steady work, every stone which they could move was out. The floor had almost disappeared underneath them.

There was no golden angel.

"Either the other walls haven't been done yet or there's no angel in this tower," said Crispin. "Do we start on the other walls?"

Joslin had collapsed on to a clear piece of floor. He was sweating and exhausted. He couldn't bear the thought. Besides: "Crispin," he gasped. "I've thought of something."

"What?" said Crispin. He seemed to be as fresh as when he started.

"Coll said that one of the builders was found stabbed to death. What if Luke had made him hide the angel and then killed him to keep him quiet?"

"If Luke could kill his own father, I don't doubt he'd despatch some poor wretch who worked for him,"

Crispin replied. "But why would Luke hide the angel he'd taken such risk in stealing and then forget where he'd put it?"

Joslin thought again. "Perhaps it wasn't Luke who stole it. Perhaps someone else took it off him, made the workman hide it and then killed him for his trouble. Now Luke has to spend his nights looking for it. If that's the case, no wonder he loses patience."

"We should go to the bailiff's house and ask him," said Crispin.

"You heard what Coll said. We wouldn't take two steps towards it and stay alive. That's no sort of ending to all our efforts."

Crispin saw sense in that. "All right. We'll start on the other walls." he said.

He stood in front of a large stone opposite and hammered a wedge into the mortar. After a few blows, the stone loosened. He pulled it out. Then he said in a strangled voice, "Look at this."

Joslin held a candle close to see what Crispin meant.

The bones of a human hand, tied to a nail fixed fast in the next thickness of stones.

They stepped back, unable to speak for a few moments. Joslin's first thought was, *no wonder Christina's hair turned white*. "Whose is it?" he managed to gulp.

Crispin did not answer. For a long time, unable to move, they stood staring at the hand. Then Crispin said, "We work on, to see the whole body. This is worse devil's work than I could have dreamed of."

"But you did dream about it," said Joslin. "Being walled up alive. The worst fear of all. The dream you shared with Christina."

Crispin didn't answer, but hammered into the next line of mortar.

"We'll be here all night and near dead at the end," Joslin replied.

"Wrong," said a voice behind them. "You'll be here a lot longer than one night, and worse than near dead."

They wheeled round to the corner where the voice seemed to come from. The draught from the tunnel entrance had disappeared. Joslin tentatively pushed his hand towards where it was. He touched cold, immovable stone.

"It's been blocked up," he cried.

"So has the other one," shouted Crispin in horror. "Quick. Up the stairs and into Luke's way out."

No use. A flat, heavy stone had been placed over the top of the steps. They could not even get to the floor above. They were trapped in a small place with the bones of someone long murdered, lit only so long as these few sputtering mutton-fat candles would last and then confined in impenetrable darkness.

Now Joslin felt every deepest fear he ever had rush in and overwhelm him.

Edwin set about his task. In the guardhouse of the castle he found fifteen soldiers with nobody in charge, bored out of their minds with nothing to do and only too pleased to be put under his command for a few hours, especially if there might be a fight. Then he went to Byster's gate and spoke to the head watchman. This weary old soldier agreed to come with his men as long as watchmen from other gates went as well. "Come back here in an hour," he told Edwin.

Edwin went back to the castle, collected the soldiers and then returned to the masons' lodge. "All right," said Hubert. "We're coming."

If the watchmen came, Edwin would have, with the masons, a small army of more than forty men. But when they came back to Byster's gate, no extra watchmen had turned up. They waited, the soldiers very impatient, until eight more watchmen from Eigne gate, Widemarsh gate, Friars gate and Owen's gate at last appeared.

Edwin surveyed his little army. The soldiers were

properly armed, the watchmen came with a few pikes, spears and memories of battles long ago, the masons had picks, shovels and trowels which, they assured Edwin, could give a nasty wound when wielded by someone who knew how to use them. Three carried axes. Edwin did not ask how many smocks and tunics hid sharp knives. If Jude Cox carried one, why wouldn't other masons? Even Ulf had a large cudgel almost as big as himself. Abel, Robin and Will were trying to make their good-natured faces look fierce. Edwin remembered what Will had said about his scar being made by a trowel and wondered how true that was.

They marched off from Byster's gate. Freya doggedly followed him wherever he went, mounted on her thin horse. Edwin sat astride his and surveyed his motley force. He regretted that it had come to this: he'd wanted to solve the murders by thought alone. He abominated brute force. But needs must. . .

"Forward, then," he shouted. "To the house of Luke Thurn and what awaits us there." His call sounded more confident than he felt. He wished he had a real knight with him, who knew about war, could direct this army properly and would know what to do when they got there.

They set off, soldiers first, watchmen second, the masons led by Hubert last, with Ulf struggling to keep up at the rear. Freya rode at his side. "I'll not go back to St Katherine's," she said. "I'll come with you."

"I wish you wouldn't," he replied. "There may be bloodshed before the day's out. It will be no place for any woman."

"I am a woman of God," she answered. "He will protect me, just as He is even now protecting Agatha."

I wish I was so sure, Edwin thought, but did not say. Of course, he couldn't order her back. She'd take no notice and their burgeoning trust and even friendship would be gone almost before it had started.

The men marched, the horses walked. The three miles seemed longer to Edwin than when he, the masons and Arthur had escorted Jude Cox' s body to Hereford. He wished the new, confident Arthur was with him. He was sure Arthur wanted to be there as well. But Arthur knew his priestly duty. After Edwin had outlined his purpose, Arthur quietly retreated into the cathedral.

What would they find? Was this unknown other who took Christina up the ladder the same who hurled Jude to his death? Why should Jude die? He seemed, as far as Edwin could see, to have done his evil work well enough to satisfy any master, Satan included. Or was this the thanks you got when you threw your lot in with such as him? What about old Coll? Would the poor fellow not last the day alive, as he feared? Above all, what about Agatha? All these thoughts wound round inside Edwin's brain, until he wondered how he expected a hastily cobbled together band of ill-armed and unsuitably cheerful men to cope with adversaries who sounded savage and merciless.

They were near their destination. To the right were the sinister rowan trees. Beyond was St Katherine's. Even now, Edwin hoped Freya might change her mind. But she kept going, looking firmly ahead.

The little army marched off the road and on to Luke's lands. Far off, the tilled land of the tenants was deserted. Trees hid the house from the road. Thick undergrowth spread by the track leading up to it.

"*Trees*," said Freya. "*Way*. Is that what Agatha meant?"

"This is the place where Coll talked to me," Edwin answered. "Then he disappeared. One moment he was here, the next he had gone. Wherever he went made a good hiding place."

"*Way in. Way to*," said Freya. "Agatha might have discovered this way, whatever it is, for herself. If Coll, as you tell me, could make himself invisible, so could she. Coll might have been doing more than merely hiding. The *way* Agatha spoke of can't be this track we're following. It's something she found. It might start here. We should stop and look."

Edwin saw sense in what Freya said. Stopping to search might be worth a try. But he looked back at his band of men itching for a fight and said, "Freya, we can't stop. I wish we could. But I have to stay in charge of this lot or they'll run riot."

"You go. I will stay," said Freya. "I'm here to find Agatha and find her I will. I believe she was here and this is where she wrote her message and sent Daw home, before anyone could see him. If it means being alone and facing whatever Agatha faced, then so be it."

"I shouldn't let you," said Edwin.

"I shall stay," Freya replied. "And there's an end of it."

Edwin knew there was no arguing. Besides, now he knew exactly what his father meant. There was so much more to this nun than met the eye. She could probably look after herself as well as any man here. "Very well, Freya. Stay," he replied. "But on your own head be it."

"Not on my head," Freya answered. "On God's."

She had tied her horse to a tree and now stood beside it as if she wanted Edwin and his men out of the way. Edwin took the hint. "March on," he ordered and the procession lumbered its way towards the house.

Soon it stood before them: the tower glared impassively. They stopped at the side of the ditch. The drawbridge was drawn up. Just as before, the building was deserted.

The men were quiet. Then one said, "Let's get across this moat and storm the place." There were mutters of "Aye, let's get on with it." "What have we come for if we don't?" Ulf's voice sounded clearly from the back. "Let me at them. I'll kill them all."

Edwin turned and faced them. "What is the point of storming the house when there's plainly nobody in it?"

"What about the cottages?" came a shout.

"People living in them are innocent," Edwin answered.

"Then why are we here? Where's all the death and devils we're supposed to wipe out?" The cry was angry. Edwin knew these men felt cheated. There must be some action soon or he would be in big trouble.

Freya watched the men go. Then she pushed on into the undergrowth. Brambles scratched her face, nettles stung her and thorns dug deep into her arms and made blood flow. She kept going. These wounds were nothing. They were like the snares and traps of the world, lying in wait for the unwary and unthinking, but which God's elect saw as nothing.

Even so, she wondered what sort of way this was. How could Agatha keep going through such wild, bloodletting tendrils?

Then, suddenly, the brambles stopped reaching for her, the thorns ceased digging into her skin. She stopped just in time, at the edge of a great chasm in the ground, lined with wood. Wooden steps led downwards. Freya breathed a prayer of thanks. This was what Agatha found, this was where Coll had disappeared to.

She pulled up her nun's habit and unflinchingly, but cautiously, made her way down. "Agatha, keep faith and be strong. I shall soon find you," she said out loud.

The sputtering of the candles which lit up this stone trap sounded like imps' sniggering laughter. Their smell, like roasting meat from feasts, mocked them. For the first few minutes they pushed and heaved at the stones blocking the ways in. Nothing moved. Then they shouted. Their voices were trapped dead and echoless in the tiny space: they knew nobody would ever hear. "Save your energy and your breath," said Crispin. "You may need it."

For what seemed a very long time they sat on the floor and said nothing. The candles burned down. Crispin lit two more from their dying wicks.

"What happens when the last one's out?" said Joslin.

Crispin didn't answer. Joslin knew. There would be no more light in his life and they would die dark, miserable deaths without air.

He couldn't just sit here doing nothing. He wanted to know as much as he could before he died. He picked up a candle and looked carefully at stones still mortared into the wall.

"What are you doing? What's the point?" Crispin muttered.

Joslin didn't answer. He was peering closely at the mortar. Then he said, "Crispin, we're wasting our time. We thought someone was only starting to search the cellar. We were wrong. This mortar's new. They were just finishing."

"I don't care," Crispin groaned. "The quest I've been on these last years is over. It's come to nothing. I'm beaten. Eleanor will never see me again and never know what happened to me."

"But this is important, Crispin. The angel isn't here. Someone else as well as you is on a useless quest. What does that mean?"

"It means nothing. I *know* it's not here."

"It does mean something. *Think.*"

"I'm past thinking."

"If it's not here, it's somewhere else. Whoever is looking for it doesn't know where. Perhaps that person thinks you might know."

"Well, I don't. How could I?"

"But Crispin, this person doesn't know that."

"Rubbish. We're left here to die."

"We can't be. How can they use their passageways if the entrances are blocked up until we starve?"

For answer, Crispin grunted. Then he said again, "Save your breath. You may need it." But Joslin felt a ray of hope. They might not be finished after all. But what would happen when the owner of the voice, the person who had closed the stone behind them, came in? *Don't admit the fear,* he thought.

But he had to admit it. Wave upon wave of suffocating terror swept down on him. He was back in that dreadful tunnel into the castle at Stovenham. The entrances would be unblocked, they'd be interrogated, tortured, their lives worth nothing. If they didn't starve slowly in darkness, they'd die quickly and bloodily in light.

He tried to hang on to hopeful thoughts, but the bad ones were too strong. Another candle went out. "One left," said Crispin. "I shall keep it, just in case. . ."

For a moment, Joslin felt happier. Perhaps Crispin hadn't given up completely. Then the darkness settled like a choking shroud, and even before Joslin had breathed twice it seemed to have smothered him for an eternity.

They kept a fear-stricken silence. Then Crispin spoke. "You're right. This is the terror Christina and I shared when we were children."

So they were both in the middle of what they feared most. No one would ever think that Crispin would feel such panic, Joslin thought. *Or perhaps someone knew perfectly well.* If that was so, what might that tell him? There could only be one answer. *Luke was doing this. So whoever was walled up wasn't Luke.*

There seemed no more to say. His mind stopped working. He wanted to pray, but no words came. He could hear Crispin's breathing. Now another memory came, from the very beginning of his time in England. He was back in a cell in Stovenham castle. He was waiting to be hanged at dawn. That night would never leave his memory – how he had stopped wondering about the wonderful new life he would make when he found his mother in Wales, because there was no hope that he would live beyond the morning. Now that feeling had come again and with it a grief and misery which bid fair to finish him off even as he crouched there.

Then he heard something. One of the stones which trapped them was being moved.

Freya was in a passage cut through earth and rock. She could not stand upright. Half stooping, half crawling, she pushed ahead because now she was down here she must keep going, even though she was in darkness. How she wished she had brought tinder. For a practical manciple not to have it was disgraceful, she thought.

Soon there was little air coming through the entrance and she found it hard to breathe. "Why am I down here?" she muttered to herself. Then she bumped her head on a hard tree root, thought of Agatha's message – "*Trees. Way*" – and remembered exactly why.

She struggled on. More tree roots scraped her head and stubbed her sandalled toes. Then she sniffed. A sudden coolness, a breath. It came from just ahead. More stumbling steps. The passage climbed slightly. She stopped and blinked. She could see light coming from over her head. She tentatively reached a hand upwards and found she could almost stand upright. More brambles scratched her. This must be another entrance hidden by undergrowth.

The passage went further. But for now, she could scramble out and see where she was. Awkwardly, she lifted herself through straggling thorns and stalks. Her face was scratched again, but soon she was in blessed open air once more.

She looked round. The house was about twenty paces away. There was a moat behind her: the passage was dug underneath it. She had come out in the last clump of undergrowth: from here to the house was open ground. Could she be seen? For the moment, she must stay hidden. She was just about to drop back down when she saw a steady pair of eyes looking at her and a mouth opened to speak.

Edwin couldn't stop them. A soldier shouted, "Look in the cottages," ran through the ditch and over the other side. Other soldiers followed. If only, Edwin thought, someone was in charge of them. He knew he wasn't. He closed his eyes in horror. There would be a blood-bath of people he knew were innocent.

The soldiers burst into the nearest cottage. Edwin heard women's screams and feared the worst. A soldier emerged, carrying something small and wrapped in cloth. Edwin shuddered to think what it might be.

But then the bundle let out a thin wail. The soldier was looking down on it with a foolish grin on his face. "It's a baby," he said.

"What have you done to its mother?" Edwin shrieked.

"Nothing," the soldier said.

A young woman came out of the cottage, tears streaming down her face. The soldier, with awkward grace, handed the baby to her. The tears stopped and she disappeared back inside with it.

"These ent no devils," the soldier said. "What are you talking about, Edwin Pendock?"

"Let's go home," said another. "There'll be no sport here."

"Aye," said another. All the soldiers formed up and marched off. The watchmen saw this and talked among themselves. Then the head watchman from Byster's gate spoke. "We reckon they're right," he said. "There's no call for us here. We've got our duty back in the city. So if you don't mind, Edwin. . ."

A moment later they, too, were crossing the ditch.

Only the masons were left. They muttered mutinously amongst themselves. But then Hubert said, "I know what I said before we came, but now we're staying. I know a bit about what's going on here, and I say Edwin needs us. If anyone thinks different he can go, but there's no job for him with me ever again."

The muttering stopped. "You're right, Master Hubert," said Robin.

Edwin, thankful that some had stayed, fell to thinking. The fields were empty of workers – and so must be the cottages if a baby could be snatched without the husband protesting. Where were they?

He led the masons on, round the house and tower. The tower stood, inscrutable as ever. The courtyard was silent.

Now the masons were restive. "What's the point of coming if there's nobody here?" one shouted.

"Whatever we're looking for lies inside," said Edwin.

"What are we waiting for, then?" This was Abel's voice. "There's a window broken. We could all get through it."

Before Edwin or even Hubert could stop them, they

were scambling though the shattered casement into Luke's solar. They stopped. "This will be the master's room," said Hubert.

They did not pause to look further but streamed out into the hall.

"It's a long time since anybody had a feast in here," said Will. He led the way further, into the kitchens and the rooms over them.

Hubert faced Edwin accusingly. "There's not a soul anywhere in this place," he said. "Why are you wasting our time?" No sooner had he spoken than Abel shouted. "What's this, then?"

The masons had found the great door barring the way into the tower. "If we could open it, I know we'd find what we're looking for," said Edwin. "But it's barred from the other side, so we can't."

"Then we'd better go back," said Hubert. "You won't have heard the last of this, Edwin Pendock."

Then Ulf's voice spoke up. "I remember my father telling me. . ."

Freya recoiled in fear. Then she remembered who she was and looked steadfastly at what faced her. A human form shadowy in the undergrowth, with features she did not expect to know.

But she *did* know them. The figure stood, shook off brambles and leaves. Freya could not keep back her joyful shout. "*AGATHA!*"

Agatha placed a finger over Freya's mouth. "Quiet," she whispered.

"What happened? We thought you were dead, ever since little Daw came back on his own," Freya gasped.

"I've heard about things done by evil men possessed. I've prayed to God to show me a light. So far He has not. But now He's shown me you and that is light enough."

"Things done by evil men?" Freya repeated. "We've seen enough of them ourselves."

"Tell me," said Agatha.

So, despite longing to hear Agatha's story, Freya told everything she knew of events since the day Christina was buried. When she had finished, Agatha said, "Does that explain any of what I saw? Listen to this, Freya, and listen well. When I left St Katherine's, I crossed into Luke Thurn's place as if I were going to call on him as a neighbour with bad news. But no sooner had Daw set foot on his land than I saw men. Think of it, Freya. Two men, crouching in a ditch, trembling and clinging to each other as if their last hour was here, looking at me as if I was the recording angel come to make them answer for their sins.

"Freya, they crossed themselves when they saw me and cowered away even more. 'Come now, fellows,' I said, 'I see you are in great fear. Tell me what ails you and I will give you God's comfort.' 'Truly, we've done great sin all right,' said one. 'But not half as great as what's been done to the other poor devil,' said the other. 'You're talking in riddles,' I answered. 'How can I help you unless you are clear with me?'"

"And were they clear with you?" asked Freya.

"Be patient," Agatha replied. "I'm coming to that. 'There was murder done here last night,' said one. 'But not by us,' said the other quickly. 'Then by who?' I asked. The first man answered, 'No, that's more than our lives are worth, to tell you. Even if you were St Peter before the gates of heaven, I wouldn't. What are we but humble masons who don't matter?' The other said, 'It's what we had to do with the body that made us into sinners.' The first man said, 'We were told that there were two particular men who would come past here today. We had to take this body and put it in the rowan trees over the road where they would see him as they passed. The sight of it would be bound to lure them in, and they were particularly wanted here because there were some old scores to settle. They'd been seen in Worcester last night, and they were bound to leave first thing, so they'd be here late morning.' 'Well, we waited over here with the body,' said the second man. 'We saw a cart going into St Katherine's and as soon as it was gone and nobody was around to see us, we dragged the dead man over the road and stuck him in the rowans. Then we waited. A few people went by, but they never saw the body stuck there in the trees.' The first man continued, 'Then we realized nobody could see him – not unless they were looking. So we pulled his arm out and let it dangle.' 'Just in time,' said the second, 'because two horsemen were coming along from Worcester way. They must be the ones, we thought. But as they came along, that cart came out of St Katherine's and they saw the arm and then the body, and made a great fuss about it.' The first said, 'There was a priest with them and he didn't like it a bit. We were worried in case they tried to take it into Hereford. Then the two horsemen caught up and when we heard what they said, we knew they weren't the ones at all. So the road was empty again.'"

"One can almost feel sorry for them in their plight," said Freya.

"Don't be," Agatha replied. "I told them the priest was Arthur Rawle. They did not care who it was. When the road was empty, they decided that with its arm lolling out, the body was too obvious. So they pushed it back in again, and then they worried because it couldn't be seen at all. So they had to keep running across the road and pulling it out again every time they thought travellers were coming from Worcester, and pushing it back when they saw they weren't the ones they were looking for. Luckily for them, there weren't many. But then they had a disaster. Just a few minutes before I arrived, the cart came back, with priest and Justice. They took the body out, put it on the cart and took it to Hereford. The men heard everything that was said. That was why they were so afraid. What were they going to say to the awful personage who did the killing in the first place?"

"A good problem," said Freya. "But theirs, not yours."

"I don't agree," Agatha replied. "I told them to move out of sight of the road and I would follow them. When we were hidden by the undergrowth, I said, 'I cannot give you forgiveness because I'm not a priest. But if you go back, tell all and throw yourselves on this murderer's mercy, then I will pray for your success.' Then we heard horses' hooves and voices on the road. The first man looked out and cried, 'It's them. One's got a harp on his back. That shows they're the minstrels.' Now they were really frightened. 'We could say they saw the body, but it didn't lure them in, it frightened them off and so we buried it because we didn't need it any more,' said the second. 'That's a good idea,' said the first. 'You will tell the truth or my prayers will not work for you,' I answered. 'And when you are forgiven because you told the truth, you must come back here where I lie hidden and be my guide in this place, because there's much I have to find out here concerning the death of our dear, departed sister.' 'We will, we will. Thank you, thank you,' they said and scampered off happy men."

"And have they come back?" asked Freya.

"They have not," Agatha answered. "By which I deduce that they did not tell the truth."

"I know who they wanted to lure inside," said Freya. "Christina's brother has returned. He is angry, he wants his rights and now he knows about Christina, he must be thirsting for vengeance."

"And where is he now?" asked Agatha.

"Somewhere here. Edwin's soldiers have come to find him and his friend the minstrel, as well as root out Christina's killer."

"Then I have seen them," said Agatha. "But they did not see me. Christina's brother looks the sort of man likely to march in demanding reasons if he sees a body outside his own home."

"The body was that of the mason who told Christina about the golden angel," said Freya. "He was in the cathedral when Christina was killed. But Arthur Rawle says the mason did not kill her."

"Why should the mason die?" Agatha mused. "Was it just the sight of a body or that one in particular which the murderer thought would be enough to ward the brother off?"

"But nobody could recognize the mason. His face was disfigured so nobody could know it. He was only identified by a scar on his arm."

"Then he must have done something to warrant death," said Agatha. "What could it be?" She thought for a moment. Then she said, "There's a dark presence haunting this place, so bound up in an evil purpose that all judgment, all idea of what is likely or unlikely, reasonable or unreasonable, has disappeared. I believe this presence has no thought for fellow human beings and sets them at naught."

Freya was silent for some time. Partly she was still overjoyed to have found Agatha, but mostly she was awed by the manner of thing Agatha had described. "Tell me what happened after those men had gone back," she said.

"I waited. Nobody came. But then I heard more voices. I saw five men, with swords, coming from the house, searching."

"You were right. Your men were so frightened that they'd told about you," said Freya.

"Of course they had," Agatha replied. "I nearly got back on Daw and galloped off. But no, I thought. Why should I? I've come here to do something and do it I will. I looked for somewhere to hide. It was then that God showed me the way in to these passages under the ground. But I realized that it was only by the grace of God that these men had not seen Daw. I crept to where I left Daw tied up and started to write my message on the saddle. But I stopped when I heard one say, 'What was that noise?' and another said, 'It's nothing. You're scared of your own shadow. We'll go back.'"

"I stopped writing, untied Daw and waited until they went. Then I slapped his hindquarters, told him to go home and slipped down into the passage. Since then I've watched and waited."

"What have you found?" asked Freya.

"I've found a lot. But I make no sense of it," Agatha answered. "All night and day I've stalked, skulked, hidden and watched, not sleeping nor eating. I've seen urgent comings and goings. I've seen another death and heard a man called Crispin accused of it."

"That's Christina's brother," said Freya.

"Ah," said Agatha, in a tone of deep satisfaction. "Then he feels the same indignation that I do over the death of a sister. He'll be a good ally. We'll need one. Whatever is happening here is coming to its crisis. The few serfs in the cottages you see as you come in are peaceable and try to work as serfs should. But they live in fear, for behind them is an iron rule. I have found that beyond, behind the trees the other side of the house and tower, there are more cottages and in the middle a larger, solid house. The old bailiff's dwelling, I believe. Men live with their women in the cottages and it is they who spread fear among the serfs and aren't afraid of killing. But they have their own fears. The source of those fears is in that bailiff's house."

"What is it?" asked Freya.

"I don't know. That person stays invisible. But he moves abroad, I'm sure. I've found one passage under the ground and I'm sure there are others. I think there's a passage from the bailiff's house to the tower, because lights showed there last night yet nobody crossed to it. Yet who can it be? Luke, the other brother? The Welsh brother-in-law? Well, arguments do occur over marriage portions. But I cannot believe it. What is happening here is beyond any family squabble."

"What shall we do?" asked Freya.

"Watch and wait," said Agatha. "God will show us what to do. Or Edwin will when he leads his men into disaster."

* * *

Joslin saw light in an entrance to the cellar. A man crawled out, holding a lantern. Another followed – and another and another. In the end, five men stood surrounding him and Crispin, two with lanterns.

"Luke?" Crispin asked in a low murmur, with a note of hope.

"Why do you think Luke would bother with you?" said one harshly.

"He's far away," said another. They laughed, mocking and grating. Crispin sat, leaning against the far wall.

One man stepped forward. Joslin knew it was Lud. He carried a long quarter-staff, intended to cudgel an opponent's brains out, and stood over Crispin. "I'm good with this," he said. "You'd better tell me what I want to hear." In the flickering light, Joslin saw an amazing thing – Crispin cowering. Lud raised the staff and brought it down hard on the side of Crispin's neck. *Thwack!* Crispin staggered, winced and Joslin winced in sympathy.

"Next, your ribs, and if that doesn't work, your head, until you're past thinking or even caring any more. Then your face, so you'll end up like another poor fellow who's met his end here."

Crispin put his hands up to ward off the next blow. His voice was weak, as if he had given in, "What do you want me to tell you?"

"Where's the golden angel?"

"I don't know."

A savage thrust with the end of the staff on Crispin's chest. He let out a bubbling gasp. "That's one rib less for God to make you an Eve with," said Lud. "Now – *where's the golden angel?*"

"*I don't know.*"

216

"I'll give you a chance," said Lud. "Christina told you."

"I never saw Christina. She was dead before we got here."

"I don't doubt that. But you knew from her, nevertheless. Even if she got someone else to tell you. What chance traveller spoke to you and made you decide to come home? Did he pass the news on?"

"All I heard was that Luke lived like a hermit, hadn't been seen for a long time and all was not well. It was then I decided to come home. I knew nothing about Christina in a nunnery."

Thwack! This time, on the side of Crispin's body, above his kidneys.

"If you're not lying, you're no use, so you're dead."

"Isn't the angel here?" Crispin's word's came out as if wrung from a damp rag.

"You know it's not. Every cranny of the tower has been searched."

"Who wants to find it?" said Joslin.

"Who asked you to say anything? A few blows with my staff can alter your pretty face, so keep quiet."

"Kill them, Lud," said one of the men.

"I'll not waste my strength. I'll keep them alive until they feel like telling us. If they don't, we'll have a better way of getting rid of them."

Joslin was determined not to die ignorant. Besides, his mind was racing: there was only one answer to this puzzle. "I know who's looking for the angel," he said.

"Quiet!" roared Lud.

"Who?" Crispin's voice was no more than a pained gasp.

Joslin would only talk to his friend. He turned away

from their tormentor. "I've worked it out. Luke's been dead for years. The person who's behind all this, who's searching for the angel, is Gwylim. Luke stole it, hid it, Gwylim wants it back. I don't blame him if it's really his."

"If Luke hid the angel, Gwylim wouldn't kill him before he'd shown him where it was," Crispin managed to say.

"He must have. There's no other explanation."

Lud stepped back. "Gwylim?" he scoffed. "If you knew how funny that was. . ." There was no doubt – he meant this.

Joslin was amazed. Who else knew about the angel? Luke stole it, hid it, Luke died and was walled up behind these very stones, then Gwylim searched for it. It followed, as night follows day. So who else could. . .?

Someone else was following Lud and the men into the cellar. Joslin saw a figure all in black: black cloak, black hood, dark even in this dark place. The figure rose, tall and straight and stood next to Lud. Joslin tried to make out features on the face.

This must be the person who wanted the angel so badly as to kill Christina, kill Jude Cox, have Hawkin killed, and probably kill Luke. And if it was not Gwylim, it was. . .

"*Of course,*" he breathed.

When Ulf started reminiscing about his father, the masons jeered.

"Not now, Ulf," said Edwin. "I'm sure your father was full of interesting stories, but now is not the time, and here is not the place."

Hubert was not having this. "Listen to Ulf, Edwin," he said. "His father was a good man and a fine craftsman. He ended up dead in a Hereford street and nobody knows why, and that's a cross his son has had to bear, which nobody deserves. So let Ulf say, his piece."

"Very well, Ulf. I'm sorry," Edwin said, feeling slightly ashamed.

"Thanks, Master Edwin," said Ulf. "Well, my father, he worked for Luke Thurn. He did jobs for him that Luke wanted kept secret-like, so my dad couldn't tell anyone. But he told me because I was his son and he knew I wouldn't blab. I've not told nobody, ever."

"Go on," said Edwin, suddenly interested.

"He got my father to build him a passage from his chamber, in between the walls, over the great hall and up to the wall at the other end. My dad couldn't see what it was for until after he'd finished, when Luke started building that great tower. Luke got a mason from out Worcester way as well, to do some other jobs for him. Nobody was to know about them and he paid them well to keep quiet. My father thought Luke Thurn was a very afeared man. . ."

"He'd be even more afeared if he thought a halfwit like you knew about it," Will shouted. The other masons laughed too, as Ulf cried, "I never told nobody till now," in an injured voice.

"How long was it after that when your father was found dead?" asked Edwin.

"Not long, Master Edwin," Ulf replied.

"I see," said Edwin. Was that why – to silence him for ever? Then they underestimated Ulf. "Where did you say this passage started?"

"In Luke's chamber," said Ulf.

Edwin knew he must find this passage, but he wouldn't go on his own. Should he take Hubert? Then who would be in charge of the masons? No, he'd take Abel, a good man he'd come to know well these last few days. And Ulf should come as well, of course, as a reward for telling them.

Hubert was quite happy to lose Ulf, less so at losing Abel. Still, he agreed. Ulf smiled broadly now he was being some use and atoning for helping, even if unwittingly, in the murder of Christina.

"Here's what we do," said Edwin. "We all go back to the room we came in. Hubert, you take the masons outside again and keep watch all round the house. If there's trouble, be ready for it. If it comes to a fight, then don't hold back. Abel and Ulf, come with me."

Back in the solar, the masons scrambled out

through the window. Edwin, Abel and Ulf searched for the passageway Ulf's father built.

Ulf found it. First, a cry of, "Master Edwin, the angel again," then a lifting of the tapestry and the sight of the steps upwards.

Edwin looked at them. A cold hand closed over his heart, with a feeling that once up these steps there would be no escape: the horror he had stalked these last days would soon be livid in front of him.

Hubert felt at a loss. He'd happily direct a thousand men when it came to building a great cathedral. But he had no idea how to deploy the few left with him when it came to being a battle leader. Besides, out here in daylight they looked what they were, masons with trowels and shovels, while nearby were men who would stop at nothing. If ever they got out alive he'd make that Edwin pay.

"Let's walk round the house like a big patrol, Master Hubert," said Will Goodlad.

"Wait till I give the orders, Will," Hubert answered. "Anyway, that's what I was going to say."

So they set off, round and round the house, through the courtyard, past the outbuildings and well, eyes darting this way and that, looking for the ambush that Hubert was sure would be upon them any moment.

Freya, behind a tree, saw their march. She whispered to Agatha, "Hubert and his men. Shall we join them?"

"Let them go," Agatha whispered back. "We'll see what they do."

They watched Hubert's band, huddled together in a tight bunch, move across the front of the house and disappear round the tower. In a few moments they appeared on the other side and did it all again. Freya counted them. "Pitiful," she said. "Is that all that's left?"

"Is this Hubert's idea of keeping watch?" scoffed Agatha. "You can see why we women withdraw from the world into nunneries. The idiocy of the men in charge of it is more than flesh and blood can stand."

"What should they do?" said Freya.

"Anything but that," Agatha replied. "Don't think we're the only ones watching them. They could be cut down without mercy at any moment. The dangerous place for them is the courtyard at the back. They can be seen from the bailiff's house. A good killing ground. All those bodies to be thrown down a deep well and never seen again."

"What shall *we* do?" said Freya. "We can't just watch it happen."

"We must go into the courtyard ourselves," Agatha replied. "We must warn them and protect them."

"We may join them down the well," said Freya.

"Not so," Agatha answered firmly. "The grace of God which guards us will see us through. Remember, this is all man's doing, not woman's. No woman would be responsible for such evil as I have seen here already. You and I, we are inviolate, beyond harm."

"If you say so, Sister Agatha," Freya murmured.

So together they went round the house in the opposite direction to Hubert until they stood in the courtyard by the well. Freya looked down it. She sniffed. "There could be bodies down there already," she said.

Hubert's men approached again from the other side. It was Robin who saw the nuns and cried fearfully, "Master Hubert, look. A spirit, a devil's shape come out of the well to haunt us. Sister Agatha's dead and gone these two days, but there she stands as if she's alive."

"Do you see what I mean?" Agatha murmured to Freya. "Poor, deluded creature." She stood tall and imposing and called, "I am no ghost. I am Mother Superior of St Katherine's and I have come to lead you to where you have to go."

Hubert's relief was tempered by his men muttering. "I'll not be told what to do by no woman, even if she is Mother Superior," said Will. Robin's fear had evaporated very quickly. "If you're really alive, you ent *my* Mother Superior," he shouted.

Agatha took no notice. She marched up to Hubert. "Master Fennel," she said. "The danger to you is over there." She pointed beyond the courtyard towards the trees and the old bailiff's house. "Every step you take is seen and soon you will pay a price."

"You'll pay it now," said Freya. Men, armed and angry, were pouring over the courtyard wall and round the outbuildings. Hubert turned and saw them. His mouth opened and closed as if he was going to shout orders. But for the first time in his life, no orders came.

Agatha never flinched. "Now we'll see who's strong," she said.

Edwin, Abel and Ulf had come to the end of the passage. In front of them were the stones of the tower. Underneath, the planks had given way to more stones.

"Now what?" said Edwin.

"I don't know, Master Edwin," said Ulf.

But Abel knew. "We're inside the tower wall," he

223

said. "There will only be a stone's thickness between us and what's beyond."

"We could push that stone out," said Ulf.

Abel looked at him pityingly in the dark. "And mortar it back in when we go?" he said. He pushed at the roof over his head. After a moment it moved. "I knew it," he said. The three of them heaved, just as Joslin and Crispin had, and soon the flagstone was up and daylight streamed down on them.

Abel left it where it was, for a quick getaway. Then they stood quietly and listened.

"Voices below," said Edwin.

They crept down each flight of steps until the only stairs left led to darkness broken by weak flickering light and the voices were clearer. They stopped, dead still, and listened again.

"What's that?" said Ulf.

In one corner crouched a tiny figure. Edwin crossed to him. It was a little boy. "Don't hurt me, master," he pleaded.

"I'm not like others here," Edwin answered. "Who are you?"

"They made me climb the walls outside, because I could get in the arrow slits and they couldn't. I had to push a flagstone across the steps to the cellar to keep the people in."

"Then you can just push it back again," said Edwin. The boy cowered away. "Do it," Edwin barked. So he did and they could hear what went on below.

The voices were raised. "That's Crispin Thurn," said Edwin. A harsher voice barked. Abel listened. "I reckon I've heard that one before," he said. "So have I," said Ulf. "You? I'd bet you couldn't remember the last one who spoke to you," scoffed Abel. "That's where you're wrong," said Ulf. "It's Lud Hall."

Abel listened again. "By the Mass, so it is," he said. "He worked for Hubert when I was a young apprentice. Hubert sacked him before he brought all us masons to disrepute with his wild ways. I never heard of him after that."

Edwin remembered too – certainly the wild ways. Though that, he thought, was a weak way of putting it. Lud Hall had been a dangerous man and far better out of Hereford than in it.

Edwin listened again. Another voice joined in – and he could tell at once that it was the most dangerous of all. He listened again. Yes, there was no doubt. Even so – "*I can't believe this*," he said.

hubert's masons stared in horror at the sudden army which faced them. Twenty against thirteen, swords against shovels and trowels. This was not what he'd bargained for. Neither had he bargained for two things which happened next. First, these attackers stopped in their rush about twenty paces away. None of his men moved, either from bravery or shock. The two parties glared at each other. Then one of his own men, a young mason named Jacob Cook, peered forwards with sudden attention and said, "Isaac? Is that really you?"

Hubert noticed one in the enemy's front ranks who looked like Jacob, but was perhaps ten years older. This man said, "Jacob, what are you doing here? Go home. I don't want you harmed."

"That I won't," Jacob replied. "I'm staying with my mates."

There was a moment's tension. Then Isaac threw his sword to the ground and said, "I'll not fight against my own brother who I've not seen for the long years I've been in this benighted place."

"You'll be sorry," said the man next to him.

"Why should I?" Isaac replied. "Lud's not here to see."

Hubert expected a furious fight to start there and then. But suddenly, something completely unexpected happened. A strange, raggle-taggle army streamed through the gate. It was led by an old man with a pitchfork. Behind him were both men and women, brandishing pitchforks, scythes and spades and dangerous with years of pent-up anger. Isaac Cook's armed men were suddenly surrounded and outnumbered, even if the weaponry was pretty poor. One shouted, "What are you doing, Coll, you old fool? Take these serfs back to their hovels and get working."

Coll answered. "Not now we've come so far. It's time all this ended. The true master's come back. We'll work for Crispin or no one at all and if you think otherwise you can kill the lot of us!"

"Ha!" said the man who'd jeered at Coll. "Shed no tears for Crispin. He'll be gone the way of his brother Luke by now."

The words might sound brave, but the men in the middle had realized that they were outnumbered more than two-to-one and that a scythe-swing or shovel-blow could do a lot of harm. Isaac kicked his sword away. "I want no more part in this," he said. "I want to go back where I came from and lead a proper life again." He left his companions, went to Jacob and the two embraced like the long-lost brothers they were.

Hubert had forgotten Agatha and Freya. But then he turned and saw Agatha's face. She was looking almost transfigured. "You see, Hubert?" she said. "How the grace of God can work?"

"I didn't expect this," Hubert replied. "I thought we were finished."

One by one, swords were dropped. Even the most obdurate watched, hesitated, and then went the way of the rest. "What future have we got here?" said Isaac. "Let's go back into the world before we've bloodied our hands so much that folk will want an end of us."

"If we're ever let," said one of his friends. "Remember why we came and who keeps us here."

"Remember the promises to us," said another.

"Remember the terrible things done in our name," said a third.

"Ah, but not by us," said a fourth.

The mason's and Coll's people watched while this strange debate went on. Hubert was amazed. "Is victory so easy?" he said.

"No," Agatha answered. "These men are evil's minions, not its begetter. The serpent's poison is not drawn. Hubert, we have work to do. Come with Freya and me."

"I'll want men of my own as well," said Hubert. He scanned his troops. Of course. Will and Robin. With Edwin and Abel already somewhere inside the tower, he felt as if the army he had brought had been gradually shelled like a nut, leaving the little kernel inside.

He called them out and they faced Agatha. "Where to?" he said.

"Follow me," Agatha answered.

Edwin, Abel and Ulf heard confused voices. Then there was silence. Edwin listened hard. No, it was not silence. He heard the grunts of a struggle. But why was nobody crying out?

Then he heard something even odder. The ring of a hammer on metal, heavy blows, almost like a blacksmith at his forge.

The ringing stopped. Then another noise, quieter, soft, insidious. To Edwin it sounded inexpressibly horrible, though he could not tell why. Especially when Abel said, "Funny time to start building things."

"What do you mean?" asked Edwin.

"Don't you know what that noise is? It's a mason's trowel. It's patting new mortar down on stone. Now it's smoothing it out."

To Edwin the sound of the blade in the wet mixture was like a snake hissing.

"Listen," said Abel. "That's a scrape where the trowel rubs against the stone." The little shriek set Edwin's teeth on edge.

"Now someone's using the trowel's handle to knock the stone into place and get it level," said Abel. The little thuds were to Edwin like a small devil knocking on the gates of hell. He blinked and shook his head. Why were these everyday sounds fraught with such horror?

Abel had a more practical question. "What can they be building down there?" he whispered.

"Voices raised, struggle, silence, blows on metal, stone new-mortared and set in place? What do you think, Abel?" asked Edwin.

"It's beyond me, Master," Abel replied.

"It means no good," said Ulf. "I'm afeared."

"Don't be. We either go back and get Hubert and the others to join us in going down there, or we go on our own. Which is it to be?"

"I don't know, Master," Abel answered.

229

"I'm afeared," said Ulf again.

Hubert had no idea where this woman was leading him. All he knew was that she made him go down a hole in the ground into a place of pitch darkness which stopped him breathing.

"I'm not going down there," Will had said.

"You'll go," said Agatha in a voice like iron, and he and Robin had dutifully done so.

Her voice came from way in front of him. "Follow Freya and me. Don't try to straighten up."

A bump on the head from a hard tree root showed him why. He suddenly rebelled against this whole foolishness. Again, Agatha's voice seemed to know what he was thinking. "Don't try to go back, Hubert. Have faith and follow."

The tall figure in the gloom spoke. Even before the first word had finished, there was no doubt.

This presence behind all that had happened, this bitter foe to everything that Crispin wanted so much, this person who had thrown innocent Christina off a high tower, who had probably done the same for Jude Cox, who had wanted Hawkin dead, who had set Edwin the greatest puzzle of his life and who had finally brought Crispin and Joslin to what would be their ends unremarked and unknown to the rest of the world – *was a woman*.

And a woman well known to Crispin.

"At last, brother," she said.

Crispin groaned. "*Madge*."

It's true, Joslin thought.

"Yes, brother," she said. "Are you not surprised?"

"Madge," Crispin protested. "I can't believe this. You were strong, fine, you taught me so much. You could stand up to Luke. I was afraid of you."

"Now you should be even more afraid of me," answered Madge.

"But why?"

"Because you went away. You left us alone with Luke, a bitter, angry, violent man who had already killed his own father."

"I suspected he had, but I didn't know it," said Crispin. "Why didn't you tell me? Why didn't Christina?"

"Why should I? If you didn't want to stay with us then you had no right to be part of us any more. I'd fight my battles on my own."

"Not on your own, surely? What about Christina?"

"*Christina.*" The contempt in Madge's voice curled round the cellar like a sharp whip. "Little lackey of her brother. 'Yes, Luke, no Luke, anything you say, Luke.' That was Christina after you went. And then Luke locked us away like penned animals."

"Why did you let him?"

"How could I stop him? Christina said, 'It's for our good, Madge. Luke knows best.' With a sister like that, what could I do? But I made life awkward for him. He never got a moment's peace from me. I knew what he was doing. Looking for a husband to get me off his hands. Well, I thought, anything to get out of that house. And when he brought that great Welsh booby Gwylim for me, I took one look and said, 'Oh yes, you'll do. I'll soon get the better of you'."

"But I've heard Gwylim was rich," said Crispin.

"I should hope he was. At least I could trust Luke not to throw me away on a pauper. Oh, I married him willingly enough, though there was no love in my heart." Madge paused. Then she said, "Understand this, Crispin. There never has been any love in my heart. There never will be." Another pause. "Except for one thing."

For the first time, Joslin spoke. "The golden angel," he said.

"It's a pity, Crispin, that your friend must share your death with you," Madge said. "He sees a lot. I could have got on well with him."

"I doubt it," said Crispin. "He'd read you like one of his ballads."

"But you'll want to know about the angel. Once I left this place I thought I wanted no more of Luke. I would not have his men escort me to Wales. When I got there, I began to covet Gwylim's greatest treasure. Yes, the golden angel, only then did I know what love was. Oh, the beauty of that shining object. The deep lustre of pure gold. I saw Gwylim's face as he looked at it – that deep, self-satisfied pleasure. *This is mine*, it said. *No one knows how I came by it: no one shall take it from me.* 'This is yours now as well, my love," he said. But I knew that he was my husband and the world thought he was my lord and master, so it would never be truly mine. '*Yet it will be*,' I said to myself. 'And when it is, I'll make sure that mine are the only eyes which will ever see it.' And now, do you know, I thought of a use for Luke. Far from never seeing him again, I told Gwylim I pined for a sight of him. Why couldn't he visit us, to see what his dowry had bought? Poor Gwylim. He would do anything to please me. So I sent word to Luke to visit us. Gwylim's men took the letter."

"So Luke came to Gwylim's and stole the angel," said Crispin.

Before Madge could answer, light dawned on Joslin. "No, of course not," he cried. "*You* stole the angel, Madge, and used Luke to bring it back here."

"Of course," said Madge. "It was so easy. One night

233

as Gwylim slept, I took the angel out of its safe place and gave it to Luke. I told him to make his way home alone. I knew he'd survive. I told him to keep it hidden, because one day I'd come back without Gwylim and we would be rich together."

"And he believed you?" said Crispin.

"The poor fool, yes, he did. I told Gwylim robbers had come secretly in the night, that they'd stolen the angel. I said Luke had surprised them as they escaped and I thought they had killed him and taken his body away, though I couldn't be sure. But I was prostrate with grief for him."

"And Gwylim believed *that*?" said Joslin.

"Of course. For a little while. More fool him. Then he became sure Luke had stolen it himself. I never argued against it. Gwylim said he would keep Luke's steward prisoner until Luke returned the angel. Well, I knew that would never be. Years passed. I waited. One day Gwylim would meet his end and I planned how it would happen. I persuaded Gwylim that the only way to find out if Luke had the angel was to confront him. So off we set with a few men, leaving the steward as prisoner. But when we reached Luke's manor – oh, what a surprise."

"The tower," said Joslin.

"Of course," Madge replied. "Already built and a crew of hard men to go with it. I remember Gwylim's shout of fury when he saw Luke, with simpering little Christina next to him. 'So, Luke, you're alive after all.' Then Gwylim looked at me and I believe that for the first time he saw the truth as I laughed in his face. He turned to look at Luke and demanded the angel. It was Luke's turn to laugh in his face. He ordered his men to seize Gwylim. They dragged him outside.

'You'll find no angel here,' Luke shouted. 'It's stoned and mortared away, where'll you'll never, ever see it.'" She paused again.

"Then what happened?" said Crispin.

"Poor Gwylim. He was always a fool. Luke's men picked him up and they. . ."

Joslin saw it happening. "Threw him down the well," he said.

"That's right," said Madge. "You see ahead. Well, then they turned on Gwylim's men, especially Lud here. Eh, Lud?"

Lud nodded impassively. "We fought them," he said shortly. "We were too many for them. They're buried behind the bailiff's house."

Crispin put his head in his hands and groaned. "I can't believe what a place of blood my home has become."

"Brother, there's more to come. My husband was dead, which didn't worry me at all. But my brother had said something which I had come a long way to hear. I felt so pleased with him for keeping it safe all this time. 'Now, brother,' I said. 'Bring me the angel so that I can see it again after all this time.' 'I'm sorry, Madge,' he answered. 'Gwylim never saw it and neither will you.' And then he repeated what he said to Gwylim. 'It's stoned and mortared away where you'll never see it.' And then he ordered his men. 'Seize my sister.'"

Madge paused. Joslin looked at Lud. His face had a strange expression on it. Madge looked at him as well, almost fondly. "But my brave fellow didn't, did you, Lud?"

"No, that I didn't," Lud answered. "If Luke had hidden his angel where nobody could find it, why didn't we know? We served him. We'd given up everything outside to be his loyal henchmen. And all that time he hadn't trusted us. It wasn't right, it wasn't what a man of honour would do. I said as much to him. But he still told me to seize his sister and I still said I wouldn't – and then I told him it was no use him telling others to do it instead, because I might do what he told me but they took their orders from me. We obey Madge now."

Madge spoke again. "Then I said, 'But I'd never keep secrets from you all. I'd trust you if you gave your loyalty to me.' Lud said, 'Hear her, all of you.' And then Luke realized he was alone and there was no hope for him. 'I'll never tell you where the angel is,' he said. 'No matter,' I answered. 'I'll find it myself, even if I have to unpick every stone of your precious tower.' And at that, he laughed. He laughed so much that I knew what I had to do. 'Stoned and mortared away, is it?' I shouted. 'Well, it won't be the only object to have such a fate.'"

"It was lucky there were a lot of masons with us," said Lud with an unpleasant snigger.

Madge said, "But I see you know already, Crispin. You've met Luke in his hiding place." She laughed, and her laughter sent icicles into Joslin's heart. "It would please me to think of you in the same place. It would have pleased Christina as well, seeing as she was always dreaming of such an end. And your friend can join you, since he's helped you so much already."

So now Crispin's worst nightmare, together with something even worse than his own, was going to meet them and see them off this earth for eternity. The thought of what it would be like until they died was too horrible even to contemplate. Joslin tried to shut it out of his mind and concentrate on *now*. What else could he do?

This narrow way in the dark seemed to Hubert to last for miles. But a tally at the back of his head told him he had taken no more than three score shuffling steps. All the while, he was conscious of this strong, indomitable nun leading them. When she stopped, it was a surprise. Will, just behind him, blundered into him. They stayed very still and strange, disembodied noises from close by reached them.

The ring of hammers on metal. Then a lower, muffled sound. But Hubert knew. "Masons are at work. What are they doing?" For some moments he listened to the same sound that Edwin was hearing and he wondered. What mad place were they marooned in?

Lud's voice ground into Joslin's brain. "We obey Madge now," he said. "Luke built his tower to guard against the day he was sure Gwylim would come marauding. But we never saw any angel. We swore so to Madge. Perhaps he was afraid we'd want it for ourselves."

"What Lud tells me, I believe," said Madge.

"And you gave your service to Madge."

"Of course." said Lud. "Luke cheated us. We have livings to make. We told the serfs that Luke was going on a journey and that all would be quiet in the house. We made Madge a home in the bailiff's house and there she's stayed since, unseen by all who don't know of her task."

"Her task?" asked Joslin.

"The angel is 'stoned and mortared'," Luke said.

"Did that mean mortared behind the walls of the tower? Those were the only stones and mortar in this timber-frame house. But if it was, none of us did it."

"How could this work be kept secret?" said Joslin. "Why didn't the serfs see you and the masons coming and going?"

"Because my good masons, with no other work to do became moles," said Madge. "A passage under the ground from house to here, another from here to road – why, I had freedom to go where I wanted with none to see me."

Crispin cast hard eyes on Lud. "If you could change your duty so easily, you should give your duty to me now," he said.

"Oh, no," said Lud. "You've no chance."

"I said I wanted an end of Gwylim and Luke," said Madge. "And these good men were equal to it. The same will come to you, all in good time. But not yet. There's more to say. You mustn't die in ignorance."

"What about poor Christina?" said Crispin.

"That little mouse? She ran, didn't she. Did she know where Luke had put the angel? Lud tried to beat out of her what she knew, but she saw what happened to her brother and ran. Where to? We looked for her in the country and towns round about, and my new men enquired after her in Hereford. But never a sign did we see. Until a nun, Sister Felicity, came to look after a sick serf. Lud allowed her to: he escorted her in, and he escorted her out again. And she let slip to him where Christina had been all this time. Not a few hundred yards away. Who would believe it! We were sure she knew where the angel was, but how were we to get that knowledge out of her? What better than to lure her up the cathedral tower and hope that up there where Hereford touches heaven – a good phrase, don't you think? – fear, awe and ecstasy together would drag it out of her. So I went up the tower with her. But when I was sure she knew nothing, then – goodbye Christina. Though not before she knew whose company she was in for her final few moments.

"And there were rumours that you were coming back, Crispin. I sent spies out to watch out for you. You were seen in Worcester with your new friend. One of my men was there, heard you in the tavern, and came back with the news. When did he arrive? The moment Jude and I came back from Hereford, with the ignorant Christina lying broken on the ground. Jude had annoyed me when it was done. 'You shouldn't have killed her,' he said. 'She didn't deserve that.' 'How dare you tell me what she deserved?' I answered. 'You know nothing about her.' I think he'd grown to like her in that nunnery. And when we returned in time to hear that you'd be passing by that very day, Jude said, 'He won't like that. If he goes into the city first and finds out, then all the powers of hell will rain on us.' 'Then he mustn't go into Hereford, must he, Jude,' I said. 'What's to stop him without a battle on the high road?' Jude answered. 'I know my brother,' I said. 'Come up to the top of the tower with me and I'll show you.'

"So he followed me up and when we were looking out over the dark land, I said, 'This will, Jude. My brother won't be able to resist coming in here when he sees your body on the road outside the house.' And before he could move, he was tipped over and floating down with all the grace of Christina a few hours earlier.' End of Jude. Tell them what you did next, Lud."

Lud sniggered. "Smashed his face in with my quarter-staff, I did. Nobody would ever know who he was."

"Would you have come in here if you had found him, Crispin?" said Madge.

"You know I would," said Crispin.

"But you didn't find him. An officious justice and a silly priest took him away. And you came sniffing back and now the King's law makes puny efforts at finding out what goes on. But they won't, Crispin. Because it's over. Now you'll know how death felt to Luke."

Madge turned to Lud. "Spikes, hammers and rope," she said. To the others, silent shadows in the background, "Mix your mortar now. Stoned and mortared away."

And now the hardest, flintiest despair smothered Joslin. "Stoned and mortared away." Almost Luke's last words. That was the manner of Luke's death and now it was to be the manner of Crispin's and his own.

Edwin, on the steps above, had still not decided whether to go back and fetch Hubert, and the insidious swish of trowels and wet mortar went on. Whatever was happening must be nearly done, yet he was afraid of what he might see. Abel and Ulf were no help, except for a mutter from Abel: "I don't like this."

Hubert listened as well, from the passage underneath. He was thinking: why interrupt honest masons at their work?

Then there was a sudden peal of laughter. Just one voice. But somehow it struck fear into him. And he looked at Agatha's dark form and heard her speak words, not of fear, but of puzzlement. "A woman. God is playing tricks on us."

Two of the silent men seized Joslin. The other two seized Crispin. Lud bound their hands and hobbled their feet. They wound cloths round their mouths so they could not speak and barely breathe. Then they threw them bruisingly to the floor.

Another man took a hammer and drove spikes into the wall, four at shoulder height, as if for a crucifixion, two below them near the floor. The ringing sound of hammer on metal filled the cellar like cracked, tuneless bells. Then the first two pulled Joslin and Crispin roughly to their feet. The men combined to tie them to the spikes, arms outstretched each side, feet bound together. Now they were splayed out against the wall. And so they waited.

The men piled stones in front of them. They placed buckets of new-mixed mortar and trowels on the floor beside them. Madge and Lud watched. "This is how Luke died," said Madge.

Joslin thought: *Christina saw her brother walled up alive. No wonder she fled. And no wonder her hair turned white.*

Now the men started laying the first line of stones. The squelch and scrape of trowels on mortar and stone was the only sound to be heard. Joslin looked down, his shoulders aching, watching his feet disappear and wincing as mortar wet his legs. He did not know what he felt: it was as though he was tranced. Already he had spoken his last word: he must wait for that final moment when the stones would reach up to his head and he would breathe air and see light for the last time.

And what then? What was there, but a dreadful hopelessness, that this time nothing could stop his fate? Except a miracle.

Squelch, scrape: stones rising slowly, unstoppably, men busily working as they would for castle, cathedral, house, it made no odds. Madge and Lud watched and watched. And now Madge could not resist it: she let out a peal of laughter, demonic, possessed, which filled the cellar for a moment and then stopped dead and left just squelch, scrape, squelch, scrape.

But in that second another voice echoed round the cellar, its speaker unseen, but certainly a woman, and it said, "*A woman. Truly God is playing tricks on us.*"

Edwin heard. He knew the voice. "Agatha," he said. Then, to Abel. "I've decided. We won't fetch Hubert."

Joslin heard. His heart leapt. Was this the miracle? For suddenly the cellar seemed full. A large woman stood there as if from nowhere, who in the gloom seemed like a giantess from fable. The same voice boomed, even louder. "I had thought this would be all man's doing and no woman would oversee such evil as I see here. But I was wrong."

"*Wrong.*" The word sounded like a bell whose echo bounced from wall to rough wall. The men stopped their work. Suddenly, their will seemed to evaporate. First one, then another, dropped his trowel.

"Pick them up," Madge screamed. "You haven't finished."

"And no more we will," said one.

"Lud," Madge shouted. "Make them."

But Lud for the moment seemed frozen with shock.

242

Edwin and Hubert knew at the same moment – it was time to go in. They arrived in the cellar together, with Abel and Ulf, Will, Robin and Freya following them. Suddenly, the cellar was too full to move.

"Be careful of Lud," shouted Edwin. "He'll have a knife."

Lud had come to and reached for his quarter-staff. He wielded it – but there was no space: he was suddenly as good as weaponless.

Edwin took one look at the wall and saw the two gagged heads with stones mortared to just below their necks, soon to be covered over for ever. "My God," he said. "The worst death to be thought of."

Hubert, Abel, Will and Robin had seized the masons, who put up little resistance. Edwin lunged at Lud. But Lud did have a knife. "Look out, Master Edwin," shouted Ulf. Lud turned. There was space to cut viciously at Ulf. The knife scored his face, the blood flowed and Ulf screamed. But Agatha cried, "I'll not have this." She raised a hand and chopped Lud down with a single blow. Then she stepped back and looked at the offending hand, amazed, as if it was not part of her.

Then Freya spoke. "Where is that woman?" she said.

Edwin looked round. There was no Madge to be seen. But Joslin knew. He made frantic sounds through his gag. Will tore it off. "Up the steps," he shouted. They seemed like the first words of a new life.

Edwin was after her at once. He charged up the steps, where daylight seemed an amazing thing. No Madge. He ran to the next floor. Still no Madge. So he carried on, up steps until he reached the top. And there he saw her leaning against a battlement.

She saw him and laughed. "I've thrown two others off high places," she said. "I must see what it's like for myself. Perhaps the devil will teach me to fly."

And then she was gone: the roof was empty, as if no one had ever been there. Edwin crossed to the battlement and looked down. He saw a black shape, oddly graceful, reach the ground. But there the grace ended and he saw the ugly gawkiness of a broken body.

When Edwin came back to the cellar, he found Lud and the other four lined up against a wall and Abel, Will and Robin busily pulling out stones until Joslin and and Crispin were free. When the last stone was removed and their hands and feet were untied, they sat leaning against a wall breathing in deep draughts of the rank air.

"Madge is dead," Edwin announced.

"Luke gone, Christina gone, now Madge. Whatever she did, she was my sister. I'm alone. But I'll heal all these breaches," said Crispin

Lud spoke. "Don't be so sure of yourself, Crispin Thurn. There are still many here who are pledged against you."

Suddenly there was another in the cellar, standing on the steps. Old Coll. "Crispin," he said, "welcome home. I bring you the sworn duty of everyone here to you as the rightful master, even those who worked against you before." He saw Lud and a look of scorn crossed his face. "Even if *you* did swear duty to Crispin, I'd tell him not to take you."

Lud spat. "I'll not give a moment's grace to that man," he said. "And nor will these here," he added, indicating the four who had been walling the two minstrels in.

Crispin spoke. "If those who served Madge truly offer me their duty with a good heart, I'll take it and be glad to," he said. "Whatever they did was in thrall first to a man sadly astray, and then to a woman sadly evil. But I'll welcome them with a good heart and expect their service, because I must start my new life in forgiveness."

"Well said, Crispin Thurn," said Agatha.

I hope your trust is not misplaced, thought Edwin.

"Now I want God's fresh air," said Crispin.

"Then we go back along the passage," said Hubert.

"I want no earthy cramped tunnel under the ground," Crispin replied. "I'll go out the way I came in. Coll will lead us."

"I will, Master Crispin," Coll said proudly. He led the procession up the steps. Abel and Will tied Lud's hands and pushed him along in front of Edwin. Joslin and Crispin together walked in the middle, in front of Agatha and Freya and with the little boy who had climbed into the arrow-slit and moved the flagstone. The four other masons followed behind. Feeling gradually came back to Joslin's and Crispin's hands and feet. Edwin and Hubert helped them down into the passage Ulf's father made. Soon they were in Luke's solar, but this time left it for the great hall and the real front door.

Outside, they stood round Madge's body. Crispin was silent. Then he said, "Though she took her own life, she must have proper burial."

Everyone looked at Agatha. To take one's life was a heinous sin.

"We never saw her die," she said. "Let her be buried properly."

"I'll have the tower pulled to the ground," said Crispin. "I'll rescue Luke's bones. I'll have the well cleaned out and Gwylim's remains found. All three will be buried together. And I'll find the angel."

"Where will you look?" asked Edwin.

Joslin thought: Madge and Lud never knew about the passage from the solar. Why not? They should have if Luke made it to escape into the tower. Unless. . . "When was the passage from Luke's chamber to the tower made?" he said, not expecting an answer.

"Ulf will tell you," said Edwin.

"My dad made it," said Ulf proudly. "Nobody knew about it. Luke started building his tower afterwards."

"And then had poor Ulf's father killed to keep him quiet," said Edwin grimly.

"Or killed him himself," said Hubert.

Ulf went on. "And Luke got a mason from out Worcester way to do some more work for him. I remember my dad saying as how Luke wouldn't let them know what each other was doing. My dad wouldn't do stonework and this mason didn't work with wood."

"Coll, you told us a mason was found dead here once," said Joslin.

"That's right," said Coll.

"I remember that," said one of the four masons. "But he weren't nothing to do with us. That was a mystery, that was."

"Another man killed to keep him quiet," said Edwin.

"It wouldn't be too hard for Luke to clear a way in from the passage to the tower when it was high enough – probably by himself so nobody knew," said Joslin. "Does that mean Luke hid the angel before the tower was built? Did the mason from Worcester do it for him?"

"Luke said the angel was 'stoned and mortared' away," said Crispin. "This is a timber-framed house. No stones or mortar in it. There's nowhere else built of stone besides the tower."

"Yes, there is," said Joslin. "The well."

There was a silence. Then everyone rushed round to where the frayed rope hung, the black water glinted and the walls of the shaft were solid stone mortared in. The rest of Hubert's masons, Madge's ex-servants and the serfs joined them. Everybody waited expectantly.

Hubert sized things up. "I reckon if the frayed end were cut off, that rope would be strong enough," he said. "Will, see if there's a good big bucket in the undercroft. There's hammers and wedges in the cellar. Get them, Abel."

They peered into the depths and a rotting, stagnant smell reached up. Hubert produced a knife, paid out rope until he was satisfied and cut it through. Abel returned with hammer and wedge. Will came back with a bucket. "It's big enough for a littl'un like Robin here," he said.

Hubert knotted the rope firmly on to the bucket handle. Robin cautiously stood in it for size, then stepped aside while Hubert placed it dangling over the well. Will and Abel kept strong hold on the windlass.

"So far, so good," said Hubert. He pulled the rope

in so the bucket was at the side, then said, "Come on, Robin lad. In you get."

Robin stepped in, then Hubert and Ulf held the rope close to the side as Robin looked closely at the mortaring. Round and round they manhandled the bucket while Robin searched, then Abel and Will let the windlass down a little and Robin searched again.

Nobody spoke. The bucket had been let down some seven feet before Robin said, "I reckon these stones are mortared in separately from the rest. They've been knocked out and put back. I'll have a look."

For the second time that day there was the ring of hammer on iron, though this ring was not trapped in a small cellar but echoed hollowly up the shaft and away. At last, Robin stopped. He began to work the stones out and when he had finished he placed them on the floor of the bucket. He reached inside the dark cavity he had made. Everybody held their breath. Then he brought something out, wrapped in sacking so wet and rotten that it fell off as soon as Robin touched it.

All could see that what he held was gold and that it was an angel.

Abel and Will winched the windlass back up. Hubert and Ulf pulled the bucket to the side. Robin got out and faced Crispin. Then he solemnly presented him with the golden angel.

Crispin took it. He looked at it for a full minute. Then he placed it on the ground. His face was twisted with anger.

"Give me the hammer," he said.

There was a gasp of horror. "Crispin, you can't. . ." Joslin began.

"Can't I?" Crispin replied. He brought the hammer down on the angel with tremendous force. Before their eyes, the body cracked in two and a wing broke off.

"Does gold split?" Crispin said.

No, gold didn't. But this wasn't gold. It was stone, which had been covered with pinchbeck, gold's base imitation, and gilded so deep and so well and so expertly that not Gwylim, Madge nor Luke had ever known.

"All this for that thing," said Crispin. "Whatever its beauty, it's an evil object."

He raised the hammer again. Then he put it down. "No," he said. "I shall leave it. It goes in the grave with Madge, Luke and Gwylim. I don't know how Gwylim came by it, but I'll make sure nobody ever sees it again."

Before he left to go back to Hereford, Crispin spoke to Coll and the tenants and to the masons who had served Madge. "All who wish to leave should go now and never return. Those who stay are welcome. They keep their land and work it and I will be a good master. Past hatreds will be forgotten. I shall find a new bailiff from among you. I will make this place a beacon for fair dealing."

There was a rumble of acquiescence.

"I shall leave you now," Crispin continued. "I shall be away for upwards of a fortnight. But I'll be back. I'm going to Coventry, but when you see me again I shall have a bride, Eleanor, and I want you to love her as she will love you."

He turned to Edwin. "Thank you for all you've done," he said. "You started this investigation and you were in at the finish. When I return we'll be good friends, you and I, because with you holding on to what is right and just, Hereford is in good hands."

"Thank you, Crispin," Edwin replied. "I shall welcome you."

He turned to Hubert. "I want you to find good men for me. There are men here to tear down the tower they spent so long building, but I want such as Abel, Will and Robin to be here as well to watch them and then to restore the house to the fine place it was. Will you do that?"

"My work on St Ethelbert's is nearly finished," said Hubert. "You'll have all the men you want and that gladly. The stones of the tower can build a new chapel, so that we won't forget what happened here."

"If Agatha permits, I would like that chapel to be at St Katherine's," said Crispin. "It should be in memory of Christina."

"For that I thank you, Crispin," said Agatha, and Freya felt happiness welling in her heart.

They were back at the inn in Hereford.

"There's something I must do before we go," said Joslin. "I have to see Arthur. We owe him a lot."

"He owes you more," said Crispin.

Dusk was falling as Joslin entered the great nave through the west door. The usual pilgrims thronged St Thomas Cantilupe's shrine and the Mappa Mundi. From a side chapel, Joslin could hear a Mass just starting. He slipped inside and knelt. The priest was Arthur.

Arthur showed no sign of recognition. But when the Mass was over, Joslin waited outside the chapel.

Soon, Arthur joined him. They went outside and walked the precincts, with the castle looming and bats flying as darkness fell.

"It's all over," said Joslin. Briefly, he told Arthur everything that had happened. Arthur listened gravely, but said nothing until the end.

"So Christina's death no longer soils St Ethelbert's," he said. "And I am restored." He paused – then: "I wish I could have been with you all."

They walked a few more paces in silence. Then Arthur spoke again. "That I'm restored is due to you, Joslin. You made me face my fears. If you had not, I would have been a lost soul."

Joslin nearly said, "It was nothing." But he stayed quiet. He knew full well that it was certainly not nothing. Instead, he said, "I leave tomorrow for Wales and my own destiny. Perhaps I'm the one who will end up a lost soul. Pray for me, Arthur."

"I shall," Arthur replied. "May God go with you."

So they said farewell, and Arthur turned away to a life with Giles Longland and Ivo de Trellick.

Next morning, they were ready early for their journeys. Crispin's Cob was saddled up and so was Herry, with panniers packed and full. Joslin wore his precious locket and felt the mysterious contents rattle inside, wondering if he would soon know what they were. His moneybelt was round his waist, Guillaume's dagger at his belt and his harp on his back. He felt ready for anything.

He and Crispin stood together in the innyard. "So it's farewell at last," said Crispin. "I shall never forget the debt I owe you."

"One day we'll meet again," said Joslin. "I'll come to

your fine manor as an honoured guest with a story of my own to tell."

"Pray God you will," said Crispin.

They mounted their horses. "I leave through Byster's gate and take the Worcester Road, the same way we came in," said Crispin. "You must take the Caerleon Road through Widemarsh gate."

Suddenly, it seemed very hard. "But we needn't part finally yet," said Crispin. "We can go through Byster's gate together. You can reach the Caerleon road through Cats Lane. We'll say goodbye there."

So they rode slowly down Bye Street, through the gate and beyond the city walls. They said nothing until they came to where Cats Lane branched off to the left. Here they stopped.

"So this is finally the time," said Joslin. "God speed, Crispin. Remember me to Eleanor and may all good fortune attend you both."

"And God speed to you as well," said Crispin.

He turned and urged Cob into a canter. Joslin watched them disappear along the road until they were out of sight.

He turned along the narrow Cats Lane, his mind full of memories of their strange times together. But soon he was heading out along the Caerleon Road and Wales was coming nearer. Past the houses he could see the mountains, faint and purple in the morning mist. On the other side of them lay his fortune, his delight, his understanding. Or his failure and death and misery. Which was it to be?

A mile outside Hereford, the unseen follower who had kept to his trail since leaving France took up the chase again. "We're near the final reckoning, Joslin.

What will it be? We'll soon know now, won't we?"

And then he carefully wrapped his cloak close to hide his sallow, pock-marked face and twisted mouth.

**Here ends the fifth story concerning
Joslin de Lay's journey to Wales**

AUTHOR'S NOTE

St Ethelbert's Cathedral in Hereford is indeed a noble building, still looking much as I imagine it was when Hubert, Abel, Will and Robin worked on it. Not that they ever did: they are figments of my imagination, as is the golden angel itself. However, the work they were doing is not imagined: the great Norman arches at the crossing did slip, threatening to make the cathedral come crashing to the ground, and about this time there was frantic work to shore them up and make them safe – with results that have lasted until today. There was also, now that the city was recovering from the Black Death, new work on the great central tower, begun in 1325. If you put a ladder up from the floor today, you would probably not be able to get through to the tower above as the characters in the story do. But while the work was going on, it would almost certainly have been possible.

And what work! With the crudest of tools these masons and labourers built vast, dizzying buildings like this cathedral all over Europe, and we've had to wait for the high-tech designs of today before anything so vast has been made again.

The Blackfriars had their friary exactly where it is in the story – but whoever owned the land it backed on to, it was not Luke Thurn. Nor was there – to the best of my knowledge – a nunnery opposite Luke Thurn's place. And if there was, it wouldn't have been called St Katherine's, because I borrowed the saint's name from a chapel in the cathedral which has disappeared long ago.

Luke Thurn's manor house may never have existed, but the little fortress he turned it into was not unknown in Britain. Many local magnates in those violent times feared attack and turned their homes into tower houses. There were a lot in Scotland, of which several have survived. There were a fair number in Wales and they certainly existed in England, though there were far fewer.

I wish to thank several people in particular for their help in getting the background to this story as right as I can make it. First is Judy Stevenson from the Collections Office of Human History at Hereford Museum. She gave me information and documents and put me on to a most important contact – Mr Ron Shoesmith, Hereford historian, who wrote the important *Hereford: History and Guide* (Alan Sutton, 1992), and who gave me much help besides, including two maps of medieval Hereford. Mrs Rosalind Caird, archivist to the cathedral, gave me much invaluable advice, not only factual, but also about which books to consult and where to find them. She also copied plans of the cathedral for me which I spent much time poring over. Without these super people, I don't know what sort of fist I would have made about setting a book in a city I knew little about when I started. Every howler and implausibility is mine, not theirs!

DENNIS HAMLEY